Evie's Ghost

Helen Peters

Also by

Helen Peters

FOR YOUNGER READERS

A Piglet Called Truffle
A Duckling Called Button
A Sheepdog Called Sky

FOR OLDER READERS

The Secret Hen House Theatre
The Farm Beneath the Water

For Freddy

First published in the UK in 2017 by Nosy Crow Ltd
The Crow's Nest, 10a Lant Street
London, SE1 1QR, UK

www.nosycrow.com

ISBN: 978 0 85763 842 7

Nosy Crow and associated logos are trademarks and/or registered
trademarks of Nosy Crow Ltd

A CIP catalogue record for this book is available from the
British Library.

Printed and bound in the UK by Clays Ltd, St. Ives Plc
Typeset by Tiger Media

Papers used by Nosy Crow are made from wood grown in
sustainable forests

1 3 5 7 9 10 8 6 4 2

PART
ONE

CHAPTER ONE

Victoria Station

"Can I have a large hot chocolate with cream and marshmallows, please?" I said to the man at the counter. "And one of those doughnuts too."

I rummaged in my bag for my purse and took out one of the crumpled notes Mum had shoved at me in the back of the taxi.

"For emergencies," she'd said.

Well.

At this very moment, my mother was on her way to Heathrow Airport with her shiny new husband, who was sweeping her off for a romantic honeymoon on the Grand Canal in Venice.

I, on the other hand, had been dumped outside Victoria Station on my own, with instructions to catch a train to the middle of nowhere, to stay with an ancient godmother I hadn't seen since I was a baby.

And if that isn't an emergency that requires a large hot chocolate and a doughnut with sprinkles, then I really don't know what is.

CHAPTER TWO

The Outskirts
of Nowhere

The train crawled towards Highfield at the pace of a dying slug. It was almost dark, and so far beyond the back of beyond that there was only one other person left in my carriage. He sat hunched over a bag of crisps, snatching them from the packet one by one and crunching them with quite unnecessary violence. I considered moving carriages, but then he might have thought I was scared of him. (Which I was, but I didn't want him to know that.)

At this rate Mum would probably be in Venice before I got to Highfield Station. And then it was still another five miles by car to the house. With a godmother I knew nothing about, except she was seventy-two years old.

"You'll like her," said Mum. "She's lovely."

Which meant nothing. It's what Mum says about everybody who isn't an actual criminal. Anyway, all her attention at the time was on the half-packed suitcase open on her bed.

"This one or this one?" she asked, holding up two floaty summer dresses. I shrugged. It was freezing in London. But in Venice, of course, it would be perfect summer weather.

"Maybe both," said Mum. "They weigh practically nothing anyway."

It wasn't meant to be like this. I was supposed to be staying with my best friend Nisha while Mum was away. But then Nisha's grandfather died and they had to go to India, so Mum decided to pack me off to my godmother's instead. I'd much rather have stayed in the flat by myself, but she wouldn't hear of it.

"You're only thirteen. I can't leave you on your own for five days. Anything could happen."

"What could happen, exactly? I've lived here my whole life and nothing's ever happened yet. Anyway, I can have friends round."

"That's exactly what I'm worried about," said Mum. And then, as I opened my mouth to argue, "Don't even bother, Evie. I'm not letting you stay on your own for a week and that's final."

So. Here I was. Happy holidays, Evie.

Big fat raindrops started to splat against the windows. There was nothing outside the train but fields and trees, all bleak and bare in the fading light. We hadn't passed a house for miles.

On the plastic table, the cracked screen of my phone lit up with a text. I grabbed it with pathetic eagerness, hoping it was from a friend. But it was my so-called godmother.

Sorry, have to attend meeting. Get taxi from station. I should be home by the time you arrive. Anna

5

Well, what a lovely welcome.

I texted Mum to inform her of this new development. Maybe she'd actually feel a twinge of guilt about abandoning her only daughter to a woman who clearly cared more about some stupid village meeting than she did about looking after me.

If Mum could drag her eyes away from her perfect new husband for long enough to check her phone, that was. Which was doubtful.

I pressed Send, but there was no signal. Unbelievable. We weren't even in a tunnel. Was this what it was like in the countryside?

I suddenly had a terrible thought. What if there was no signal at Charlbury? If I had to spend five days cooped up in a random old lady's flat with no way of communicating with the outside world, I would literally die.

The rain was lashing down now, making long diagonal streaks on the windows. I thought about getting my sketchbook out to draw it, but then the train started to slow down.

Highfield. This was it.

Nobody else got out. The station was deserted. But there was one cab parked on the kerb. I walked towards it and the driver opened his window. I gave him the address, trying to sound as though I gave instructions to taxi drivers all the time. He nodded but didn't say a word, which was really creepy. I couldn't believe my godmother was actually ordering me to get into a car with a complete stranger. But I couldn't see a bus stop anywhere and there was still no signal on my phone. So I didn't really have a choice.

Within about a minute we left the houses behind and there was nothing beyond the rain-streaked windows but darkness.

The driver stayed silent. All I could see was his thick neck and the back of his bald head.

What if he wasn't taking me to Charlbury at all, but to some deserted place where he was planning to kill me and bury my body?

After what felt like hours, he turned on to a narrow winding lane. There were no other cars on the road. I felt sick with fear. I kept my fingers curled around the door handle in case I needed to make a quick getaway. He didn't look very fit. Maybe I could outrun him. Otherwise I'd have no chance.

The car slowed down. I thought I was actually going to throw up. I said frantic prayers inside my head. I'm not religious, but there was no one else to turn to.

He turned off the lane on to a narrow, tree-lined driveway. In the light of the headlamps, I saw a huge old house at the end of the drive.

"Charlbury House," he said, slowing to a halt in front of it.

I felt weak with relief. I paid the fare – half my emergency money gone already – and got out of the cab. The wind was so strong that I could hardly open the door. I still felt shaky with fear, even though there was nothing to be scared of any more.

The rain was pelting down. A gust of wind

whipped my hair across my face. As the taxi drove away, I pushed the long dark strands out of my eyes and looked up at the house.

It was *massive*. A huge, ancient, spooky stone mansion. Enormous windows with carved stone frames, and a grand flight of steps leading to the biggest front door I'd ever seen.

How could Mum have forgotten to mention I'd be staying in a mansion?

I walked up the steps, bumping my case behind me. A light came on above the front door, illuminating slanting rods of rain. Raindrops bounced off the stone slabs. There was a big puddle right in front of the door, where the stone had worn down.

Screwed to the wall beside the door, looking completely wrong on the ancient stones, was an ugly modern row of bells and an intercom. I pressed the bell for Flat 9.

I waited for ages but there was no answer. I pressed the bell again, harder this time.

Nothing. Either the bell wasn't working, or she was still not home from her meeting.

Honestly. You'd think she might have made a tiny bit of effort, instead of leaving her goddaughter standing in the rain while she sat in a nice warm room wittering on about the village scone-baking crisis or whatever it was that was so much more important than collecting me from the station.

Unless I'd pressed the wrong bell. I pulled my phone from my pocket to check the address.

But my hands were cold and wet, and the phone

slipped through my fingers. I tried to grab it, but my fingers closed around thin air and my phone splatted right into the middle of the puddle.

"Oh, no, no, no!"

I fished it out of the water and wiped it frantically on my coat, but my coat was soaking too, and the phone was just getting wetter. I unzipped my coat and tried to rub it dry on my top.

A beam of light shone on the front door and I turned to see a sports car speeding up the drive. It veered sharply in front of the steps, throwing up gravel all around it, and braked next to the house.

Somebody got out of the car and crunched briskly across the gravel. The person bounded up the steps, and I saw it was a little old lady. But not a normal old lady. She wore orange baseball boots with black trousers and a red jacket, and a broad streak of her silver hair was dyed bright pink.

"Are you Evie?" Her voice was clipped and businesslike. "You look very like your mother. I hope you haven't been waiting long. I thought I'd be home earlier, but these councillors do love the sound of their own voices. Never use one sentence when you can use ten, that seems to be their motto."

I said nothing. I was staring at her hair.

"Do you like it?" she asked, pulling out the pink strand with her thumb and forefinger. "I was tempted to dye the whole lot, but it takes a lot of work to maintain it, apparently. I might still do it at some point though. It's very cheering when one looks in the mirror, I find. Distracts from the wrinkles. Now, where's my key?"

As she rummaged in her shoulder bag, I looked at her jewellery. Enormous earrings, a huge necklace and a vast number of heavy-looking rings on her slim fingers. Her nails were painted silver.

From the depths of her bag, she pulled out a key ring in the shape of a skull.

"Are you Anna?" I asked, trying to adjust the image I had formed in my head to this pink-streaked, orange-booted, silver-nailed reality.

"I am. I suppose I should have said. What's wrong with your hand? Have you hurt it?"

"It's not my hand," I said, withdrawing it from inside my coat. "My phone fell in that puddle. I was trying to dry it."

She frowned at the screen. "The water will have got in through the cracks. It's probably dead. No great loss. The reception here's terrible anyway."

"It'll be fine if I put it on a radiator," I said, seething. How dare she tell me it wasn't a loss?

She unlocked the front door and I followed her in. The inside of the house was much less fancy than the outside. Standing in this hall, you wouldn't have known you were in a mansion at all. It looked just like the communal hall of our block of flats in London, only bigger. Same chipped magnolia paint, same pile of junk mail, same dog-eared notices on the wall.

Anna led the way up a staircase with an ugly brown carpet, threadbare in the middle. We climbed two flights of stairs to the second-floor landing.

"Here we are," she said, stopping outside a white-painted door with a lopsided brass number nine screwed to it. It opened on to a corridor with several doors leading off it. Anna opened the nearest door.

"This is the living room," she said. "Also the kitchen and dining room."

Seriously? I thought. She expects me to live in *this*?

"It's not very tidy, I'm afraid," she said, not sounding the least bit bothered, "but I've never been interested in housework. Such a waste of time, don't you think?"

OK, I admit I've said similar things to Mum many times, when she's having one of her regular rants about me leaving stuff all over the flat and never clearing up after myself and blah blah blah.

But this place…

Well.

The sofa, the chairs, the table, most of the floor and all the kitchen surfaces were buried beneath piles and piles of papers and pens and folders and magazines and books. Empty mugs and crumb-strewn plates teetered on top of every pile.

I was suddenly struck by the thought that this was probably what our flat would look like if Mum didn't clear up after me.

"I don't cook much," said Anna breezily, following my eyes to the hob heaped with books. "Things on toast mainly, and I tend to eat in bed. One of the perks of living alone. You won't mind getting your own meals, will you? I don't know what sort of food you like, but you can go to the shop tomorrow and choose for yourself. I expect you cook a lot, with your mother out at work."

I never cook. Mum always cooks when she gets home. But I didn't say this. I couldn't decide whether to be offended that Anna was clearly not planning on making the slightest bit of effort to look after me, or excited at the idea of living on crisps and chocolate for a week.

I laid my poor phone on the radiator. And then I noticed something truly disgusting.

"That's not ... real, is it?"

"My skull?" said Anna, smiling at the hideous toothy monstrosity grinning at me from the middle of the dining table. "Yes, he's perfectly real. I call him Yorick. A useful reminder, don't you think, of our mortality. None of us will be here very long, and when we're gone that will be all that's left. I should have taken him to that council meeting tonight. It might have encouraged them to hurry things along a bit."

"What was the meeting about?" I asked, trying to take my mind off the skull and thinking how interesting it was that Mum had conveniently forgotten to mention the fact that my godmother was completely barking mad.

"Well, the part I went along for," said Anna, her whole face lighting up, "was actually very exciting. There are new houses being built on this lane, and when they were digging the foundations, the builders discovered an old paupers' burial ground – a graveyard for people who couldn't afford a private funeral or who weren't buried in the churchyard for other reasons. There are hundreds, perhaps thousands, of skeletons. The oldest remains may go back to the twelfth century. I can't wait to get started on the dig."

I stared at her. "You're going to dig up graves?"

"Well, not personally. The archaeologists do that. I just examine the skeletons."

"You examine dead bodies? For fun?"

She laughed. "Not just for fun, though it *is* fun. I'm a forensic anthropologist."

"A what?"

"Essentially, I examine human skeletons to find out things about the person: their age, sex, how they died and so on. It's a fantastic source of information on how people lived and died hundreds of years ago."

"But aren't you… I mean… I thought you'd be … retired?"

"Why would I retire, when I love my work and I'm good at it? I'll take you to see the dig, if you like. Actually, you'll be able to see it from your bedroom window."

Oh, good. That was something to look forward to. I gave her a look that I hoped expressed my feelings, but she didn't seem to notice.

"I need to go and do some work in my room," she said, "but make yourself some supper if you're hungry." She gestured vaguely at the kitchen cupboards as she left. "Help yourself to anything you want."

I opened the cupboard above the hob. It contained a box of teabags and three mugs. The one next to it was empty except for a sticky jar of Marmite and several tins of sardines. I'd never eaten sardines in my life and I wasn't about to start now.

In the final cupboard was half a loaf of stale bread. The only things in the fridge were a small carton of milk and a piece of smelly cheese. There wasn't even any butter, and what's the point of bread without butter?

I decided to take a photo of the empty fridge. I needed to record my pitiful new existence. It might be useful evidence when my mother and her husband were put on trial for child cruelty.

Then I remembered. I took my phone off the radiator and tried to switch it on. Nothing happened. It was completely dead.

I tried not to panic. It just needs a bit more time to dry out, I told myself.

The silence was getting me down. I looked around the room for the TV.

A rising sense of panic built up inside me, followed by numb horror.

No. It couldn't be true.

But it was.

There was no TV.

How could a room so full of stuff have literally not one thing in it that a human being actually needed? It was like I'd gone back to medieval times. I had literally nothing in the world, and I was practically an orphan, abandoned by my utterly selfish mother and sent to a crazy old skull-loving woman with no phone, no TV, no computer and no food.

I took out my book, but I couldn't concentrate on reading. I looked around the room and saw nothing but endless hours of boredom stretching ahead of me.

So this, I thought, was to be my life for the next four days. Sitting alone in total silence, eating stale bread and Marmite in the company of a human skull.

CHAPTER THREE

The Writing
on the Window

I had just finished my bread and Marmite when
Anna reappeared.

"I just realised, I haven't shown you to your room,
have I?"

No, I thought, you haven't. You are literally the
worst hostess in the history of the universe. But I
didn't say anything. She might have thrown me out
of the flat, and then I'd have been homeless as well
as phoneless.

I picked up my case and she led me down to the
far end of the corridor, where she opened a door,
flicked the light switch and gestured for me to go in.

Unbelievable.

This room was even worse than the rest of the
flat. And I wouldn't have thought that was actually
possible.

It was dark and gloomy, even with the light on,
and it smelled of damp. The walls were a nasty,
faded shade of brown. The curtains were thin and
fraying. A bare light bulb hung from the ceiling.
There was a stained, moth-eaten rug on the scuffed-
up floorboards. And the only piece of furniture was

16

an ancient-looking iron bed, bare except for a lumpy mattress.

"I never use this room," Anna said. "Nobody's slept in here for years."

Great. That made me feel a whole lot better.

She gestured to an unbelievably dull-looking old pamphlet lying on the mattress. "That's a history of the house," she said, "in case you're interested."

I just about managed to stifle a snort.

"I'll find you some sheets," she said, and disappeared.

I walked over to the window, which was the only nice thing in the room. It was wide and tall, with a carved stone frame, and the glass was divided into dozens of tiny panes. Outside it was pitch dark. I couldn't see a thing. Which was a relief, since the room apparently overlooked a graveyard where the bodies were being dug up.

As I reached out to close the curtains, I noticed a cluster of scratches in one of the panes near the bottom of the window. Scratches that looked like writing.

I crouched down and peered at them more closely. It *was* writing. The letters were curly and old-fashioned.

Sophia Fane
Imprisoned here
27th April 1814

The hairs on my arms prickled. Imprisoned? In this

room? Why would somebody have been imprisoned in here?

I stared at the writing for a while, trying and failing to make sense of it. Then I remembered the pamphlet Anna had left on the mattress. It was called *A Brief History of Charlbury House*. I picked it up and skimmed through the pages, looking for a mention of Sophia Fane, but I couldn't find anything about her.

Anna came in, holding a pile of crumpled bedding.

"Do you know anything about that writing on the window?" I asked.

"Oh, yes," she said, dumping the bedding on the mattress. "There's quite an interesting story there."

"What is it?"

"Well, Sophia was an only child, and her father, Sir Henry Fane, apparently arranged a marriage for her with a very wealthy friend of his. Sir Henry was in a lot of debt, you see, so he needed Sophia to marry a rich man to restore the family fortunes. But Sophia fell in love with one of the gardeners instead. And when her father told her she had to marry his friend, she refused. So he locked her up in her room until she repented."

I felt myself turning cold. "In here?"

"Yes, apparently this was Sophia's bedroom. Well, part of her bedroom, I imagine. The rooms were all altered, of course, when the place was turned into flats, but this must have been her bedroom window. The legend has it that when she was locked up, she scratched those words and the date when she was imprisoned into the glass with her diamond ring."

"So did she repent?"

"Not as far as anyone knows. Anyway, she was already engaged to the gardener. Her father didn't know that, of course, but he soon found out."

"How?"

"Well, it turned out that when he locked her up, she was already pregnant."

"Pregnant? So what happened to the baby?"

"Apparently the baby was taken away from her while she slept. It was a little boy, they say. Nobody knows what became of him."

I imagined Sophia waking up one morning and discovering her baby was gone. I imagined her pleading to know where they had taken him, and being met with stone-faced silence. How awful must that have been?

"What happened to Sophia afterwards?"

"That's the strangest thing of all," said Anna. "Nobody knows."

"What do you mean? Somebody must have known. Her father must have known."

"There are all sorts of rumours, and there have been ever since it happened. Some people say she ran away and changed her name. Obviously there were no photographs in those days, so it was quite easy for a person to create a new identity without being traced. But other people think she was kept locked up for the rest of her life, and died of a broken heart. There's even a rumour that she was murdered by her father."

"Murdered? In this room?"

"It's all just speculation," Anna said, "because nobody has ever known the truth. But whatever happened to her, she was never seen again, and she was the last of the Fane family. After her father died, the house passed to a distant relative who kept it as a country retreat, but hardly ever used it. It wasn't lived in properly again until it was turned into flats a few decades ago. Right, I'll find you a towel. And is there anything else you need?"

Yes, there is, I thought. Several things, actually. A decent bedroom. My phone. My own home.

"No, thanks," I said. "I'm fine."

CHAPTER FOUR

The Girl in the
White Nightdress

I turned over in bed and shook the pillow again. The pillow was hard and lumpy and the duvet was thin and lumpy. The mattress was chilly with damp. I was freezing cold.

The clock on the living-room mantelpiece had struck eleven a while ago, but I couldn't sleep. Since Anna had told me the story of Sophia Fane, I couldn't stop thinking about her, locked up in here, grieving for the baby who was stolen from her while she slept.

There was a hideous moaning, whistling sound coming from behind the wall opposite the bed. It had freaked me out so much earlier that I'd made Anna come and listen to it.

"It's just the wind in the chimney," she said. "There would have been a fireplace there, you see, before the house was turned into flats. The fireplace was blocked up but the chimney's still there behind the plasterboard."

It didn't sound like wind in the chimney. It sounded like a pack of ghosts, howling in the walls. It was the most horrible sound I'd ever heard.

I turned over again and thumped the pillow. The ghosts in the chimney howled even louder.

As if this room wasn't uncomfortable enough already, when I took out my things to get ready for bed, I realised I'd forgotten to pack any pyjamas. Anna insisted on lending me a nightdress. I didn't know nightdresses still existed. I thought they'd died with the Victorians. It was made of white cotton and came down to my ankles, with buttons at the front and a high frilly collar. It felt really weird to wear, and it smelled weird too. A strange, old-fashioned smell.

A high metallic strike made me jump. But it was only the living-room clock. It struck twelve, and the last stroke faded away.

And as it faded away, the wind stopped whistling in the chimney. The water stopped gurgling in the pipes. The breeze stopped rustling in the trees.

I had never known such silence. It was as though the world was holding its breath.

I realised I was holding my breath too. I forced myself to breathe.

The howling in the chimney started again: a terrible, desolate, lonely, wailing sound. I covered my ears with my hands.

Tap, tap, tap.

I screamed. Something was rapping on the window.

I burrowed down into the bed and pulled the duvet over my head, whimpering with terror.

The wailing grew louder. Skeletal fingers knocked on the glass. Tap, tap, tap.

My teeth were chattering and I shivered uncontrollably. I thought I might die of fright. I wanted to run but I couldn't move.

Tap, tap, tap.

I made myself breathe. It was just a tree branch, tapping against the window, I told myself. There must be a tree outside the window.

I couldn't just lie there whimpering all night. I had to be brave. I had to go and see.

I forced myself to get out of bed and walk across the pitch-black room. I held my breath and pulled the curtains open.

A girl in a white nightdress was staring in at me. A girl with long dark hair and a desperate look in her eyes.

I shrieked and jumped back, my blood pumping, my heart racing.

Then I realised. It was my reflection. It was just the nightdress that had scared me. I wasn't used to seeing myself in a nightdress.

I forced myself to look again. My reflection looked back at me.

Except ... it didn't look *exactly* like me. And it didn't look like a reflection.

Don't be stupid, I told myself. Of course it's your reflection.

From somewhere outside the house came a whirring noise. And then another clock started to strike, with a deep, resonant sound that lingered in the air.

That was strange. I had heard the living-room

clock strike every hour this evening, but I was sure I hadn't heard that other clock before.

The clock continued to strike. And my reflection raised its hand.

What?

I hadn't raised my hand. Had I?

Then the hand…

No. It couldn't have done.

I was stone cold. Goose pimples prickled all over my body.

I must be going mad, I told myself. I must be hallucinating.

Because I was sure the hand had *beckoned* to me.

Had I just beckoned without knowing it? Was that possible?

Ice-cold with dread, I raised my arm.

The girl in the window didn't raise hers. She just stared at me with a pleading look in her eyes. As I lowered my arm, flooded with terror, she reached hers towards me and beckoned again.

"Help me," she mouthed.

I screamed, yanked the curtains back together and ran from the room. There was no way I was going back in there. No way I was staying in this flat. I would wake Anna and make her take me back to London, back to my own home, right now, this minute.

As I ran through the doorway, I had the weirdest sensation. For a moment, I felt as though I ceased to exist. It was as though my body had dissolved into thin air.

Then, as the door slammed shut behind me, the sensation faded and I felt solid and whole again. It must have been some sort of fainting fit, I thought, only without the toppling-over part.

But something was different. My clothes felt different. I looked down.

What the...?

Instead of Anna's nightdress, I was wearing a long brown apron over a long grey dress and black boots. There was a tightness around my ribcage, as though I had some sort of corset underneath the dress.

What on *earth* was going on? Was it a dream? But I hadn't fallen asleep. Had I?

I needed to wake Anna. I had my hand on her bedroom-door handle when suddenly I stopped and stared.

All the doors in her flat were modern and white, with cheap-looking handles in a dull-coloured metal.

But this was a door of polished wood, elaborately carved and panelled, and instead of a cheap chrome handle, my hand was clutched around a sphere of shining brass.

Still clutching the doorknob, I looked up and down the corridor.

Everything was different.

The doors were all of carved and polished wood, with gleaming brass doorknobs. The walls were no longer a dirty cream colour, but a lovely deep blue. Instead of the nasty brown carpet, I was standing on a beautiful patterned rug that ran right along the middle of the corridor. Around the edges of the rug, polished floorboards gleamed in the light of flickering wall lamps.

I was trying to take this in when Anna's bedroom door was flung violently open, knocking me into the opposite wall. A thin, tight-faced, middle-aged woman wearing a long grey dress marched out of the room. Her eye lit on me and she frowned.

"Are you the new housemaid?" she asked in a strong French accent. "What are you doing up here? Did Mrs Hardwick send you?"

I stared at her, speechless. She tutted. "Another brainless idiot," she said, shaking her head. "Where does she find such hopeless girls? Get back to the kitchen. Polly is on fires tonight."

I didn't move. I *couldn't* move. The woman gave me a shove in the small of my back, propelling me down the corridor.

"Get along with you, girl. This is no time to stand around dreaming."

Head spinning, I walked away from her down the corridor.

I pinched my arm as hard as I could.

It hurt.

But I already knew it would. Because this didn't feel one bit like any dream I'd ever had. Was I having some kind of crazy hallucination? Or had I gone completely mad?

CHAPTER FIVE

Polly

I opened the door that should have led out of Anna's flat to the landing. It did lead to the landing, but the landing was different. The walls were white now and the brown carpet had gone, leaving bare wooden boards.

In a fog of confusion I gripped the banister rail and started to walk downstairs. The boots rubbed my toes, and whatever was on my legs itched like mad. I hitched up my dress and saw that I was wearing long thick woollen socks. And my hair was different too. I put my hands to my head. My hair was pinned into a tight bun.

I couldn't even begin to make sense of this. My brain was unable to form a single coherent thought.

Delicious food smells wafted up the stairs and there was a distant clatter of pots and pans. As I got further down, I could make out muffled voices among the other noises.

At the bottom of the staircase was a stone-floored passageway with three doors leading off it. I was trying to decide which one to go through when the door behind me swung open and a huge hand grabbed my arm.

I shrieked, whirled round and found myself facing a man dressed like one of the footmen on Cinderella's coach. He stank of body odour.

"Let go of me!" I said, trying to shake off his hand.

He tightened his grip. "What on earth do you think you're playing at?" he said, almost knocking me out with his terrible-smelling breath. "They've been wanting you in the scullery for hours."

At least, I think that was what he said. His accent was so strong that it was hard to make out his words. Also, I was distracted by his hair, which was long and grey, and curled like a judge's wig. And yet his face didn't look older than a teenager's.

"Nell's been taken sick," he said. "Cook needs you to do the pots and pans. Have you finished the bedrooms?"

I gaped at him dumbly. "Er…"

"Are you half-witted?" he said. "Stop gawping and get yourself to the scullery if you still want a job in the morning."

"Er … where's the scullery?"

He shook his head, as though he couldn't believe what he was hearing.

"Follow me."

He led the way down the passage and I took in his extraordinary clothes. He wore a dark-blue velvet tailcoat trimmed with gold braid, velvet knee-length knickerbockers, stockings and gold-buckled shoes. It really was like he'd just stepped out of a fairytale.

He opened the door at the end of the passage and

led me into an enormous old-fashioned kitchen. It was boiling hot. A big open fire burned in the centre of a massive black oven. A great long wooden table ran down the middle of the room. At the far end of it, a fat woman sat in a high-backed armchair facing the fire.

"Take those knives to the pantry, Alice," she snapped to a skinny, exhausted-looking girl in a filthy apron. "And all the dirty pots to the scullery."

"Yes, missus," muttered the girl, collecting up an assortment of lethal-looking knives from the huge table. The woman heaved herself up from the chair with a groan. As the girl passed her, the woman, for no reason that I could see, hit her on the side of the head. The girl whimpered and disappeared through a doorway, past another girl scraping food scraps into a metal bucket.

"And don't you even think about going to bed before this place is cleaned until it shines," called the fat woman, hobbling out of the kitchen. "I'm off to my room. My legs are fair murdering me."

"Not surprising, with all that weight on them," muttered the girl scraping plates, as soon as the woman was out of earshot. I laughed and she looked up. She had a lively, expressive face and I liked her straightaway. She looked about my age, and she was dressed exactly the same as I was.

Her eyes widened with surprise when she saw me. Then she turned to the curly-wigged man, raised her eyebrows and gave him a sly grin.

"Ooh-er, George, this your new fancy piece?" She

had the same strong accent as he did.

"Give over, Polly Harper," he said. "You mind your cheek."

Polly winked at me.

"You'll be the new girl then," she said. "You took your time."

The girl in the dirty apron came back through the door. "This is Alice," said Polly. "She's the kitchen maid."

Alice shot me a look of such hatred that I turned around to see who was behind me. But there was no one. That look really had been directed at me. What had I done?

Polly didn't seem to have noticed. "And this is the new housemaid," she said to Alice. She turned to me. "What's your name then?"

"Evie."

"That's a pretty name."

Alice scowled.

"Foreigner, she be," said George. "Addle-pated too, I shouldn't wonder. Probably dropped on her head as a baby. I'll leave her to you, Polly. I've got better things to do than stand around making introductions."

He left the room and Polly nodded her head in the direction of the door in the corner. "Scullery's the first door on your left," she said. "Best get started on those pots and pans if you want to get to bed before midnight. I'm off to check the bedroom fires. I'll come and see how you're getting on in a bit."

According to the big clock on the wall, it was

nearly eleven. But for me, it was well after midnight and I suddenly felt exhausted. I had no idea what was going on but I wished it would stop. I pinched myself again, as hard as I could bear. It hurt, but nothing happened.

The scullery was a small room, lit only by one weak lamp. The wooden draining board that ran all along the far wall was piled high with dirty pans and utensils. If they were expecting me to wash up that lot at eleven o'clock at night, they had another think coming.

"So you've arrived at last," said a harsh voice.

I wheeled around to see a broad-shouldered, very upright woman standing in the doorway. Her grey hair was scraped back in a tight bun and a huge bunch of keys hung from a chain at the waist of her plain black dress.

"Well, have you nothing to say for yourself?"

I stared at her. What did she expect me to say?

She raised her eyes to heaven and shook her head. "So, I've been sent another halfwit. Where do they find these girls?"

"I'm not a halfwit," I said.

"Oh, so you can speak when you choose," she snapped. "We'll be having none of that chat from you, missy. When I speak to you, you say, 'Yes, Mrs Hardwick.' The rest of the time, save your breath for your work. Is that clear?"

"Yes, Mrs Hardwick," I parroted with heavy sarcasm.

"Evie, is it?"

"Yes, Mrs Hardwick." My sarcasm was wasted on her. She didn't even seem to notice.

"And your surname?"

"Tregarron."

She wrinkled her nose as if the word had a nasty smell. "Funny name, Tregarron."

"It's Cornish," I said. People often comment on my unusual surname. "There's only one family with that name. They came from this tiny Cornish hamlet."

Mrs Hardwick frowned. "You haven't travelled from Cornwall, surely?"

"No, I'm from London. My family left Cornwall hundreds of years ago."

"Well, you look clean and strong enough. Show me your teeth."

"What?"

"Come along," she said with an impatient gesture. "Open your mouth."

"What? Who are you, a dentist or someth— Aarrgghh!"

As I was speaking, she actually lunged for my mouth and pulled my jaws apart. I tried to bite down on the bony interfering fingers, but her hands were unbelievably strong. After a few seconds, she withdrew her fingers.

"Good teeth," she said. "You'll do. No more of your cheek, mind. Cocky little madam, aren't you? But we'll soon work that out of you."

She started to walk out of the room.

"Mrs Hardwick," I called.

She turned. "Well?" she snapped.

"I'm not doing this washing-up now. It's too late and I'm tired. I'll leave it to soak and do it in the morning."

And by the morning, I thought, hopefully everything will be back to normal and I won't have to deal with it.

Mrs Hardwick took a step forward. The expression on her face actually scared me.

"What did you say?"

Her voice was very quiet. Quiet and deadly.

"I said I'll do it in the morning."

In a flash, she lifted her hand and smacked me hard on the side of my head. I stared at her, open-mouthed, tears springing to my eyes from the shock of it.

"You hit me!" I shouted. "You actually hit me! That's against the law!"

In response, she smacked me again.

"I don't know what sort of situation you've come from, young lady," she said, her blue eyes icy, "but in this house, servants obey their superiors. Now, get on with your work."

And she walked out of the room, leaving me gaping after her.

My head throbbed and my neck ached where the slap had jarred it. Please let this be a dream, I prayed. Please let me wake up now.

I pinched my arm. It hurt, but it didn't wake me. But it *had* to be a dream.

I looked at the disgusting heap of washing-up. Maybe I could just run away.

I went to the door and tried to open it. But it was bolted and padlocked at the top and bottom. I tugged uselessly at the bolts.

"Had enough already?"

I turned to see Polly standing in the doorway. She laughed.

"Can't say I blame you. This your first position?"

"Er…"

"Your first time in service?"

I looked at her blankly. "I don't know what you mean. I don't understand any of this. I'm not meant to be here. I don't even know where I am."

She looked sympathetic. "Taken from the workhouse, was you?"

"No! I was taken from my mum. But I'm staying with my godmother. I don't know how I ended up here."

"Oh, that's tough," said Polly. "But don't worry. There's worse places to work. How old are you?"

"Thirteen."

"Same as me. It's murder at the beginning, but you'll get used to it. You won't usually have to wash pots, that's one blessing. It's only when there's a big party on, we have to turn our hands to anything then. And what with poor Nell taking sick…"

"Who's Nell?"

"Scullery maid. Just standing at the sink she was, and fainted dead away. No wonder – she'd been washing pots and pans for six hours without a break. I tell you straight, I'm right glad they don't give parties too often. And I'm glad you turned up

34

too. I'm rushed off my feet doing the bedrooms, without this lot to wash as well."

Polly was so nice that she made me feel a bit calmer. Maybe it wouldn't kill me to do a bit of washing-up. Just this once, obviously. I might as well get on with it and just hope that things went back to normal very soon. I really didn't fancy spending any more time in this dream, or nightmare, or hallucination, or whatever crazy madness it was. But if I thought about it too much, I would completely freak out. So perhaps it would be better to have something to keep me occupied until the madness went away.

There were two sinks in the centre of the draining board. One seemed to be made of stone and the other was lined with metal. But there were no taps anywhere.

"Er ... Polly, where do I get water from?"

"Cold from those buckets there," said Polly, indicating two metal buckets full of water on the floor under the sink. "Hot from the copper on the range."

"And the washing-up liquid?"

Polly looked at me as though I was speaking a foreign language.

"Come again?"

"The washing-up liquid. Where is it?"

"You don't half talk funny," said Polly. "Down from London, are you?"

"How did you know?"

"Well, you're not from round here, are you?" She looked curiously at my face. "You look too healthy for a Londoner. What you doing in Sussex? Is there no work in London these days?"

"No, it's just... Well, my mother got married and she didn't want me around, so she sent me to the country."

Polly made a sympathetic face. "Hard luck."

I wasn't sure whether her sympathy was for my mother's callousness or for my having to come to the country, or both. But either way, it was nice to feel that somebody cared.

I asked for the washing-up liquid again, speaking as slowly and clearly as I could, and trying to make my accent sound like Polly's. But she still didn't understand. So I just said, "What should I use to wash the dishes?"

Polly bent down and opened the cupboard under the sink. She took out a bowl filled with a gritty-looking paste. I dipped my finger in it tentatively and sniffed. It smelled of vinegar.

"What is it?"

Polly stared at me. "Have you never washed pots before?" She glanced at my hands. "Those hands don't look like you've washed pots. They're lady's hands, they are." Her look of curiosity turned to one of sympathy. "Fallen on hard times, have you? Come down in the world?"

"A ... a bit, yes."

"Oh, that's a shame," said Polly. "Don't you worry now. I'll look after you."

She stood the bowl of paste on the windowsill behind the sinks. "Sand, salt and vinegar, that is.

The copper pans come up lovely with that and a bit of elbow grease. That's only for the outsides, mind. You do the insides with this." She pulled out another dish. "Sand, salt and soap."

"Is there a brush?"

Polly opened a drawer full of rags. "Cloths in there. Come and get yourself some hot water."

She picked up an empty bucket and I followed her to the kitchen. On one side of the fire was an enormous copper tank with a tap at the front. "Fill your bucket here," she said. "I've been topping up the copper all evening, so there's plenty of hot water. Dry the pans as you go along. There's drying cloths in the scullery. Then you put them back on the shelves." She pointed to the wide shelves running along both sides of the kitchen, with dozens of gleaming copper pans on them, arranged in size order. "In the right places, mind, and upside down, so the insides don't get sooty. And leave them hanging over the edge a bit to let them air. You'll catch it from Cook if you don't do that. Now, I need to go and see to the bedroom fires, or Hardwitch will skin me alive."

"Hardwitch?"

"Mrs Hardwick. The housekeeper. A right piece of work, she is. Have you not met her yet?"

"Oh, yes," I said bitterly. "I've met her all right."

Polly laughed and scurried out of the kitchen. When she reached the door, she turned. "I'm glad you're here, Evie. It won't half be good to have another pair of hands around the place. It's been hell since Eliza went."

I stared after her, light-headed. This must have been how Alice in Wonderland felt when she tumbled down the rabbit hole. I wanted to make sense of things but it was impossible.

So I didn't even try. Instead, I turned off the tap on the copper and picked up the bucket. It weighed a ton. I lugged it out to the scullery, put the plug in, heaved up the bucket and poured the hot water into the sink.

CHAPTER SIX

The Ball

As I stood in front of the dark, curtainless window, scrubbing my way through the mountain of pans and utensils, I heard people bustle in and out of the kitchen. There was more washing-up going on in another room nearby; I heard the rattle of cutlery and occasional bursts of men's voices, singing or laughing. One of the voices might have been George's. But nobody came into the scullery.

My eyelids began to droop. I could almost have fallen asleep right there, standing at the sink. Only the stinging pain in my hands from the sand and vinegar kept me awake.

"Psst. Evie."

I turned to see Polly in the doorway, her eyes full of mischief.

"Do you want to go on an adventure?" she whispered.

"What sort of adventure?"

"Upstairs. To the Great Hall. We'll just peek around the door. They'll be so drunk by now they won't notice."

Even though I was exhausted, I couldn't resist the

idea of spying on an actual ball. It would certainly beat washing-up. And since I had somehow ended up in this crazy situation, I might as well play along with it for the moment.

I patted my sore hands dry on a tea towel and followed Polly up the stairs and along a wood-panelled corridor. As we moved closer to the babble of noise, I heard violins playing classical music, almost drowned out by the sounds of talking, laughter and clinking glasses.

Polly stopped by the open door of the Great Hall. "Follow me," she whispered. Not that anyone would hear her above the noise.

I stayed close behind her as she darted around the doorway and pressed herself against the wall behind a wooden screen. She crouched down and indicated for me to do the same. The wood was carved into a sort of lacy pattern, so when we pressed our eyes to the holes, we got a pretty good view into the crowded room.

It was such a kaleidoscope of colour and light and movement and sound that it was hard to pick out details at first amid the whirl of costumes and dancing and music and voices. And the smell was like nothing I'd ever smelled before. Woodsmoke, candles, flowers, spices and strange musky perfumes all mixed with the powerful stench of body odour.

The women looked amazing. They wore low-necked, high-waisted long silk dresses, with beautiful sashes and embroidered bags and shoes. They carried lace fans, and their jewellery sparkled in the candlelight.

On a carved wooden balcony at the far end, a group of musicians played, and down the centre of the room a line of couples danced an old-fashioned country dance. In a corner by the huge log fire, older people played cards at little candlelit tables.

George, the grey-wigged man who had frogmarched me into the kitchen earlier, and another man dressed identically to him, were clearing a long table under the window, collecting up the remains of puddings, a couple of chicken carcasses and dirty dishes strewn with meat bones. The sight of the puddings made my mouth water. I had eaten nothing since that stale slice of bread and Marmite in Anna's flat. I couldn't believe that was only this evening. It felt like it was in another world. What in the name of all the planets was happening to me?

Polly nudged me and pointed. "See that fat man with the blond hair and red face, standing by the table there?"

I nodded.

"That's Mr Ellerdale," she murmured. "Friend of Sir Henry. They say he wants to marry Miss Fane."

Miss Fane. Why did that name sound familiar? Then I remembered, and a shiver of recognition ran through me.

"Miss Fane?" I asked. "Sophia Fane?"

Polly nodded.

Ideas and questions flooded into my head, jostling for space, one pushing forward and then being shoved aside by another, making me dizzy.

All this crazy stuff that was happening to me ... was it somehow all connected with the girl at the window? Could that girl have been Sophia Fane?

The girl had asked me to help her.

I went cold all over.

Was that what had happened? Had I gone back in time to help her? To change her fate?

But that was crazy. Completely ridiculous. People didn't travel in time.

And yet ... look what was happening to me right now.

But it couldn't be time travel. It just couldn't. However real it all seemed, it had to be some sort of dream. It just had to. All the upheaval – Mum getting married, and being sent away, and Anna's weird flat, and the story of Sophia Fane – all of that must have just caused me to have some incredibly vivid dream.

Polly's voice broke into my thoughts. "Mr Ellerdale's filthy rich. Owns half the county, they say."

So this was the man Sophia's father wanted her to marry.

I studied Mr Ellerdale. He was talking to a thin, worried-looking woman while brandishing a large bone, tearing strips of meat from it with his teeth between guffaws. He wore shiny black riding boots over tight, flesh-coloured trousers, and his great fat stomach was practically bursting out of a navy-blue tailcoat.

As Polly and I watched him, his eyes lit on somebody

near our screen. He called out and raised his hand in greeting, almost knocking the thin woman off her feet. Either he didn't notice or he didn't care, because he tossed the bone on the table and strode across the room as if everybody else in it was invisible. Polly and I adjusted our positions, and I saw that he was heading towards a short, wiry, middle-aged man with bristly red hair, a misshapen nose and flushed, broken-veined cheeks.

"Who's the red-haired man?" I asked Polly.

"That's your master," said Polly. "Sir Henry Fane."

Sophia's father. I scrutinised his face. Did he look evil enough to lock up his daughter and take her baby away?

"Where's Sophia?" I whispered to Polly. "Is she here?"

Polly looked shocked. "Miss Fane," she said. "You must always call her Miss Fane."

"Miss Fane then. Is she here?"

Polly squinted through the holes. "I can't see her at the moment. I'll tell you when I do."

A stern-looking dark-haired woman in a blue velvet dress and a glittering diamond necklace wove her way through the throng towards Mr Ellerdale and Sir Henry. People moved aside for her with little greetings, bows and curtseys, which she received with slight nods, as though she was the queen.

"That's Mrs Bailey," Polly whispered. "Sir Henry's sister. Came to live here after Lady Fane died. You don't want to get on the wrong side of her."

Mrs Bailey gave a slight curtsey to Mr Ellerdale,

and he made a deep bow in return, the brass buttons on his jacket almost popping under the pressure.

"Excellent ball, this, Henry," he said.

"It should be," grunted Sir Henry. "It's cost me enough."

"Sir Henry, really!" scolded his sister. "Now, where *is* Sophia? She has been *so* looking forward to seeing you tonight, Mr Ellerdale."

Mr Ellerdale bowed low again. "It will be the greatest of pleasures to further my acquaintance with your charming niece, madam."

Sir Henry's eyes searched the room, frowning. Then his eyebrows shot up, his cheeks flushed even redder and he made a strangled, gargling sound.

Polly nudged me so hard that I almost toppled against the screen. She grabbed my arm to steady me. "There's Miss Fane," she whispered.

The gaggle of people at the table had thinned out to reveal a girl sitting on a window seat, wearing a white dress. Was this the same girl who had appeared at my window? It was hard to tell. The girl in the nightdress had had long wild hair and a desperate expression on her face. This girl's dark hair was swept up on her head in a fancy do. And she looked the opposite of wild and desperate. Unlike everyone else in the room, she wasn't talking or flirting or playing cards, or even watching the action. She was completely absorbed in a book.

"*Reading!*" Sir Henry burst out, a look of disgust on his face. "By the devil, after all I've told her…"

He looked as though he were about to combust.

He took a step towards Sophia, but Mrs Bailey put a hand on his arm. Her expression was grim.

"Leave this to me, Sir Henry," she said, and made her way through the crowd. When she reached Sophia, she stood directly in front of her, with her back to us, so I couldn't see either of their faces.

Two old ladies moved close to the screen, fanning themselves.

"I know it is none of my business," said one of them, "but even if I were reduced to begging on the street, I should not like to think I should be so heartless as to sell my daughter to Charles Ellerdale."

Her friend laughed. "You may say that in your situation, Louisa, but I wonder whether, should you really be reduced to penury, your sensibilities would remain quite so fine."

"That poor child," said Louisa. "Barely sixteen years old, and he must be over forty."

"It would never have happened if her mother were alive," said her friend. "God rest her soul, she must be—"

"Shh," said Louisa, as Sophia's aunt, her lips tightly pursed, headed back through the crowd, grasping Sophia's arm. Sophia looked furious as she stopped in front of the two men and gave a brief, stiff curtsey to Charles Ellerdale. He bowed in return.

"Good evening, Mr Ellerdale," she said in a flat monotone.

"Miss Fane, what a very great pleasure." He grasped her hand and kissed it. "Would you do me the very great honour of standing up with me for the next two dances?"

Sophia said nothing, but she let him take her arm. She had rearranged her face into a blank mask.

They walked towards the centre of the room, where several couples were lined up facing each other. The men bowed to their partners, the women curtsied and the dance began. The couples moved towards each other. Mr Ellerdale trod on Sophia's toe and she winced.

He stepped back and bumped into a young woman standing behind him. She stumbled, and the drink in her glass splashed down the front of her dress. The man standing next to her turned to Mr Ellerdale and said something. Although we were too far away to hear their words, I could tell by the look of surprise and anger on his face that Mr Ellerdale had said something rude in response.

I looked at Sophia to see how she was taking it. And when I saw her expression, my heart stood still.

Mr Ellerdale turned back to her with an ingratiating smile, and her face became a blank mask again. But, for a few seconds, I had seen the mask slip. In those few seconds, the expression on her face had been desperate.

And now I knew for certain.

The girl at my bedroom window was Sophia Fane.

CHAPTER SEVEN

The End of the Day

Polly grabbed my arm and hauled me upright. "Come on, Evie. I need to check the bedroom fires, and you must finish those pots, or we'll both be for it. I'm supposed to be training you up."

I couldn't imagine anything worse than scrubbing more pots right now, but I didn't want to make trouble for Polly, so I followed her back to the scullery.

It was freezing down there after the heat of the ballroom, and by the time the pans were finished, my feet ached, my head throbbed and my hands were rubbed raw from the sand and stinging horribly from the vinegar. A red stain was coming off my fingertips. When I took my hands out of the water to dry the pots, I couldn't believe it. It was blood, seeping through my skin.

Polly popped her head around the door.

"You done, Evie?" She picked up a drying cloth. "Let's get these last few pots dried and go to bed. You look dog-tired."

"Look at my hands!" I said, holding them out. "They're actually bleeding."

Polly gave me a sympathetic smile. "Hurts something rotten, don't it? But don't worry, they'll soon toughen up. You'll grow a hard skin, like mine."

She held out her hands. They were rough and red and covered in lumps and calluses.

"Not very pretty, are they?" she said. "Rough as sandpaper. I'll never get a husband with hands like these. But at least they don't hurt as much as they used to. Now, did Hardwitch show you your room?"

"No."

"You're sharing with me. Where's your box?"

"Box?"

Polly's eyes widened. "Ah well, never mind," she said cheerfully. "At least you'll be earning here. You'll be able to buy another set of clothes before long."

Buy another set of clothes? I had a flash of panic. What if I actually had travelled to the past? What if I couldn't get back?

No. That was ridiculous. I couldn't have travelled to the past. It wasn't possible. It must just be a really vivid dream. It couldn't be anything else.

From a cupboard, Polly took out two candles set in tin saucers and lit a splinter of wood from the embers of the fire. She lit the candles and handed one to me. I followed her through the hall and up the stairs. The lamps had been put out and our candle flames were the only light. They made long, spooky shadows on the walls and they gave off a smell like rancid meat.

48

Up and up we climbed, to the very top of the house, where a narrow green door so low that I had to duck to get through it opened on to a low-ceilinged passage. Polly led the way to a door at the far end.

It opened into a small room with a sloping ceiling. There were two narrow iron beds with white covers. Between the beds stood a table with a large bowl and jug on it. There was a little wooden chair and a tiny window with a thin curtain. The white walls and the rough floorboards were bare.

Polly set her candle on the table, sat on the bed and started to unlace her boots.

"Where's the bathroom?" I asked.

Polly frowned as she tugged at a lace. "The what?"

"The bathroom."

Polly laughed. "There's no bathroom here. What sort of place are you used to?"

"Oh ... er ... but ... where do you go to the toilet?"

She frowned again. "The what?"

I searched my brain. What word would they have used in those days?

"The WC?"

"I haven't the foggiest idea what you're talking about, you funny London girl." She reached around to the back of her dress and untied her apron.

"The lavatory?"

"Oh!" Polly laid her apron over the back of the chair. "What odd words you use up in London. There's a servants' privy behind the stables, but you can't go outside now. George will have bolted all the doors. But there's a chamber pot under your bed."

A chamber pot? Did that mean what I thought it meant?

I bent down and lifted the blanket that hung over the side of the bed. Sure enough, there was a big white china potty sitting on the floor.

No *way* was I using that.

I stiffened in horror as a thought occurred to me. Polly wasn't going to use hers, was she? Not while I was in the room? Please, no.

Under her dress, Polly wore a corset. I must be wearing one too, I thought. That would explain the tightness around my chest.

Over the corset, Polly had something tied around her waist – a length of ribbon with a flat fabric pouch hanging from it. She untied it and slipped it under her pillow.

"What's that?" I asked.

Polly frowned at me in bewilderment, as though she couldn't believe my ignorance.

"It's my pocket, of course," she said. "Do you not have a pocket?"

I smoothed my hands down the sides of my dress. There was an opening on each side. Through the slits, I could feel my own corset and, tied around my waist, a piece of ribbon with two fabric pockets attached to it.

"I do have pockets!" I said, and then wished I had sounded slightly less delighted.

Polly gave me a look that made it obvious she thought I wasn't quite all there. To be honest, I didn't blame her.

I felt inside my pockets, but they were empty. I wondered what Polly kept in hers that was so precious it had to be hidden under her pillow at night. I wanted to ask her, but then I'd probably have sounded even more stupid.

Polly was undoing the fastenings on her corset. I would never be able to undo all those buttons and hooks with my sore and bleeding hands. But I couldn't ask Polly for help. She already thought I was an imbecile. Anyway, all I wanted to do was sleep.

I set my candle on the bedside table, sat on the bed and started to take my hairpins out. That hurt my fingers too. But lying on hairpins all night would be even worse.

"Evie!" shrieked Polly.

I jerked upright. "What— AARRGGHH!"

Icy water cascaded over my head and down my dress. I leapt from the bed.

"What are you doing?" I shouted. "Are you mad?"

I pushed aside the dripping curtain of hair plastered to my face and glared at her.

"Is that your idea of a joke or something?"

"Your hair was on fire," she said. "I had to put it out. Sorry."

But she didn't look sorry. She started to laugh, and her laugh was so infectious that I started laughing too.

"Your face!" she said. "Your face when you glared at me through your hair!"

"Was it really on fire?"

"Of course it was. It was dangling in the candle. Look."

She lifted a section of dripping hair from the side of my head. One part of it was several centimetres shorter than the rest.

"Oh, no!" I wailed. "There's a great lump out of it!"

I touched the blackened ends. They came off on my fingers.

"Never mind," said Polly. "It won't show once you put it up. You need to take more care with your candle though."

"I can't sleep in these clothes now. Everything's soaked."

Polly crouched down and pulled a rough wooden box, about a metre long, from under her bed. It was padlocked. She pulled her pocket out from under her pillow and took a key from it. So that was what she kept in there.

"There's another shift in here," she said. "We'll hang your clothes over the chair to dry."

"Thank you," I said, as Polly handed me a long white nightshirt. I put it on and flopped down on the mattress. I didn't care how hard and lumpy it was. Never in my life had I been so grateful to go to sleep. It had been the weirdest night of my life. But I was too exhausted even to wonder what was going on any more. All I could do was hope against hope that I would wake up in the morning in Anna's flat and this would all have been a dream.

CHAPTER EIGHT

Thirteen
Years Ago

Light filtered through the curtains. The mattress was hard and the pillow was lumpy. The sheets smelled weird. My feet ached. I was wearing something strange.

My heart jolted as images flooded into my head. Polly ... the ball ... the washing-up ... Mrs Hardwick ... the girl at the window...

I sat up and stared around the room. My suitcase lay on the floor where I had left it, the contents spilling on to the rug. The bedroom door was flat and modern and painted white.

With a hammering heart, I got out of bed and opened the door.

Dull cream walls. Horrible brown carpet. Ugly radiator.

Everything was back to normal.

So it *had* been a dream. An unbelievably vivid dream. So vivid that I wondered whether I had actually gone back in time.

I felt relieved, obviously. But, weirdly, a part of me was a little bit disappointed. I definitely hadn't expected to feel that. But it *would* have been amazing to be able to travel through time.

I walked back into the room and closed the door. My fingers hurt as they pressed the handle. I looked at them.

My hands were red and raw, and covered in little cuts.

A strand of hair fell over my face. It smelled weird. It smelled *burned*.

I stared at it numbly for a minute. Then, with shaking fingers, I pulled the hair on the left side of my face in front of my eyes. My stomach lurched as another strange smell hit my nostrils.

Vinegar.

My head started to throb. With a hammering heart, I spread out my hair in front of my face like a curtain.

In the centre of the curtain was a gap, where one section of hair was several centimetres shorter than the rest of it.

My hands shook as I touched the shortened ends. Bits of dry, blackened hair crumbled off on my sore fingers. I stared at the desiccated flecks. My legs felt weak. I plonked myself down on the bed.

So it hadn't been a dream. It had really happened. I really had travelled back in time.

I didn't know what to think. My head was spinning so much that I *couldn't* think.

A knock on the door made me jump.

"Evie?"

"Yes?"

"Oh, you are awake," Anna said, coming in. "I

was almost starting to worry."

"What time is it?" I asked, looking for my phone. And then I remembered.

"Nearly eleven," Anna said.

"Eleven! I never sleep that late."

"Well, you must have needed it. And you must be hungry too. There isn't much food in the house and I need to walk to the burial ground for a site visit, so I thought, if you came with me I could point you in the direction of the village shop. And I could show you round the burial ground, if you like."

"Er, thanks?" I said. "But just the shop will be fine."

My phone was still completely dead. I asked Anna if we could go to a repair shop but she said she wasn't going into town today.

"I could get a bus," I said.

"You could. The next one's on Tuesday."

I stared at her but she didn't appear to be joking. She looked at me and laughed. "You really are a London girl, aren't you? You're in the country now, Evie. Things are different here."

Oh, you don't have to tell me, I thought. You have no idea how different.

It wasn't tipping down like it had been the previous day, just drizzling in that depressing way that makes the whole world grey. On either side of the driveway was a strip of grass, bordered by wooden fences. Behind the fences were modern houses. "The gardens were supposed to be gorgeous in the old days," said Anna, "but nearly all the land was sold off for building when the house was converted into flats. There's just this bit of lawn left now, and a little patio at the back. They kept the lovely old gates though, and part of the original wall there."

I suddenly remembered something.

"Is there a clock in the gardens? I thought I heard a clock strike last night, outside the house."

Anna shook her head. "I don't know what that would have been. There's a clock above the old stable block but it hasn't worked for goodness knows how long. Certainly not in the time I've lived here."

We walked through the wrought-iron gates, and I remembered how scared I'd been last night when the cab driver had turned in here. So much had happened since then that it felt like a lifetime ago.

We turned left, down the narrow, tree-lined lane. The trees were dank and dripping. Fat drops of water splatted on my head and ran down my face. I rummaged in my bag for a tissue.

"That's a pretty bag," said Anna.

"Thank you." I was quite proud of my bag, which I'd made from some of Mum's leftover curtain fabric.

"It looks hand-sewn," said Anna. "Did somebody make it for you?"

"Yes," I said. "I did."

And she actually looked impressed.

"How could I find out more about what really happened to Sophia Fane?" I asked.

She seemed surprised. I tried to look as though I

was just very interested in history.

"Your best bet would be the local records office," she said. "That's where the old church records of births, marriages and deaths are kept. But nobody seems to know much for definite about Sophia Fane, so I can't imagine there's a lot to find."

"Can we go to the records office?"

Anna looked at me curiously. "Of course, if you'd like to. It's not open at weekends, but I could probably arrange a visit next week."

"Thank you," I said. "That would be great."

She smiled. "I'm glad you're interested in history. Your mother never mentioned that on the phone."

"Too busy drooling over her perfect new husband, probably."

She raised her eyebrows. "Oh, yes. She did say you were finding it a little difficult to accept the idea of a stepfather."

Oh, did she, indeed? Thanks very much, Mum. I wondered what else she'd been saying about me behind my back.

I shrugged. "Well, I've never had a father, have I? My dad left before I was born, and Mum and I have always been fine. We don't need anyone else around."

Anna frowned. "Are you sure your mother feels the same way?"

"Why shouldn't she? She's got me."

She gave me a sideways glance. "So, this new stepfather – he's trying to push you aside, is he?"

"Well, he's taken Mum to Venice without me, so

yes, obviously."

"You wanted them to take you along? On their honeymoon?"

I made a disgusted face. "No, obviously I didn't want to go on honeymoon with them."

"But you're angry that your mother's gone away without you."

"She's my mum. Mums are supposed to stay with their children."

"And your mother goes away a lot, does she?"

What was with all these questions all of a sudden? What had she and Mum been talking about?

"Not a lot," I said.

"But she's neglecting you, is she, now she's got Marcus?"

The mere mention of his name irritated me. Well, it's an annoying name, isn't it?

"No," I said. "She's not neglecting me."

"And he's horrible, is he, this Marcus? Selfish, cold-hearted?"

"No." She was *really* annoying me now. I wished she'd go back to ignoring me.

"So?" she said. "What's the problem exactly?"

I let out my breath in exasperation. "He's just ... always there, you know? Being annoying."

"So his crime is to have fallen in love with your mother."

"Exactly. Why couldn't he have left us alone? We were fine before."

Anna smiled. "It can't be easy, when it's just been the two of you for so long. But you need to see it from her point of view. Can you imagine how lonely she must have been these past thirteen years?"

"Oh, thanks," I said. "Thanks a lot."

"I know she has you, and I know she adores you, as you know full well yourself. But adults need adult company sometimes, just as children need the company of other children."

"She's got loads of friends."

"I'm sure she has, but it's not quite the same. It wasn't easy for her, you know, giving up her degree and having you so young. And with no help or support from her mother either, after your grandmother suggested having you adopted."

I froze. "Having me *what*?"

Anna stopped walking. She looked horrified. "I thought you knew. Oh my goodness, I'm so sorry."

I felt hollow inside. "What do you mean, having me adopted?"

"I shouldn't really say anything. It's up to your mother to tell you."

"Well, she's not here, and you just told me, so you'd better tell me properly now."

Anna didn't speak for a few seconds. Then she started walking again. "There's nothing much to tell, really. You know your mother was still at university when she had you. Her mother had been very ambitious for her, and she thought Lara should have you adopted so she could carry on with her studies unhindered, as she put it. Well, Lara wouldn't hear of that, and they had a huge falling-out. Lara refused to ask her mother for any support after that, which made things very difficult for her. I don't imagine she's had a lot of trips away in the last thirteen years, has she?"

None at all, actually. But Anna probably knew that already, since she seemed to know everything.

"And then her mother died before she had a chance to make things better," said Anna. "Very sad. But your grandmother hadn't had an easy relationship with her own mother, and unfortunately these things often repeat themselves in families."

It was raining hard now. Raindrops pattered like drumbeats on the leaves above us and dripped down on our hair and clothes.

"I invited your mother to come here and live with me when you were born," said Anna. "Did she tell you that?"

"Really?"

I didn't mean to sound quite so surprised, but Anna didn't seem like a person who'd enjoy sharing her space with a mother and baby.

"Well, I have a spare room, and I'd known her since she was a little girl, so it was the least I could do. But she only stayed one night."

I didn't blame her. I was surprised she'd stayed at all, once she'd seen the state of the place. Mum's a very tidy person.

"She was in a terrible state, poor thing. You were so tiny, and she was exhausted. She had terrifying nightmares about a mother and child being separated. Well, not exactly nightmares, more like hallucinations, I suppose, because she claimed she never went to sleep at all."

Suddenly I felt cold all over.

"What did she see?" I asked, and my voice came out all weird, like there wasn't enough air in my throat.

Anna looked at me in surprise. "I'm not scaring you, am I?"

I shook my head. Anna smiled. "There's nothing for you to worry about. It was only natural, I suppose, that your mother was having nightmares about a separated mother and child, considering what she was going through."

"What did she see?" I asked again. "In these hallucinations?"

"She said she heard a baby crying next to her bed. It must have been you, of course, but in her state of exhaustion she was convinced it was the ghost of a long-ago baby. And she said she heard a tapping at the window, which must have just been a branch, but she thought it was the baby's mother, knocking on the windowpane."

"Did she ... did she see who was tapping at the window?"

Anna looked at me incredulously. "Evie, we're three floors up. How could anyone have tapped at the window? It was just the wind knocking a branch against the glass."

"But did she go and look?"

"No, she was far too scared. She ran into my room in hysterics, with you clutched in her arms. She said she couldn't stay in there for one more second."

"What time was it, when she ran out of the room?"

Anna laughed. "It was thirteen years ago, Evie. I'm afraid I can't recall that level of detail."

But I had to know. I had to.

"Was it before or after midnight?"

"I really can't—"

Then she stopped.

"Actually, I do remember. It's funny you should say that. She said afterwards that she'd just heard midnight strike when the noises started. I said the striking of the clock must have half woken her and she must have been in some sort of strange state between dreaming and waking. But she wouldn't go back in there. I gave her my room instead."

"Had you told her the story about Sophia Fane? Had she seen the writing on the glass?"

Anna shook her head. "No, I don't think she saw the writing. She wasn't in the room long enough, and she was preoccupied with you anyway."

"And when you swapped rooms, you didn't ... hear anything ... in the spare room? Or see anything?"

"Not a thing. Slept like a baby. And I've had various guests over the years, who have all slept perfectly well in there too. Poor Lara. She wrote to me afterwards to apologise, poor thing. She said she'd been exhausted and sleep-deprived, and she couldn't believe she'd got herself into such a state." She looked at me with concern in her face. "You look stricken, Evie. Honestly, there's no need to worry. It was only a dream."

CHAPTER NINE

Double Midnight

At the entrance to the burial ground, I parted from Anna and continued to the village alone. I walked along the lane very slowly, my eyes to the ground, thinking.

So the ghost appeared at midnight. That is, the normal midnight, when Anna's clock struck twelve. That was when it had appeared to me last night, and when Mum had heard the tapping, thirteen years ago. But Mum hadn't gone back in time and, somehow, I had.

Did Mum run out of the room before the second clock struck midnight? The clock that apparently didn't work any more, but presumably was working two hundred years ago? Was it this phantom second midnight that transformed the house into how it was back then? Could that explain how Mum heard the ghost at the window, but didn't go back in time?

Or was it that Mum didn't actually go to the window and see the ghost, so it couldn't beckon her into the past like it did to me?

Suddenly, with a strength of feeling that took me by surprise, I really, really wanted to know what was going on. That night, I decided, I would stay awake until midnight and see if the house transformed again.

I was terrified of being in my room at midnight. The thought of going through that again made me feel sick. But now that I knew Mum had had the same experience, I wasn't quite as scared as I had been before. At least I knew I wasn't the only freak in the world.

And I really wanted to see more of the house two hundred years ago, and the people who lived there.

Most of all, I wanted to find out more about Sophia Fane. Because a question was worming its way into my head.

Sophia's ghost had begged me to help her. So if I had the power to go back in time, did that mean I might be able to change the past?

It's amazing how much junk food you can buy in one small shop. If Mum could have seen the contents of my basket, she would have died of horror.

Anna gave me money for food so I didn't have to spend my emergency fund. I did spend some of it though. Polly had said I wouldn't normally have to wash up, but I wouldn't have put it past that savage Hardwick woman to make me wash a load more pots and pans purely for her own sadistic amusement. I wasn't going to put my hands through that agony again for anything, so I bought a pair of rubber gloves. If I didn't have to wash up, I could give them to the poor scullery maid. I couldn't imagine how sore her hands must be.

On impulse, I also bought a box of chocolates for Polly. I took the gloves and chocolates to my room as soon as I got home, so that Anna wouldn't see them and ask awkward questions. Although she wasn't back yet anyway. Too busy getting excited about skeletons, clearly.

My phone still wasn't working. It was spookily quiet in the flat and I felt very alone. I unplugged the radio in the kitchen and took it to my room. Then I got out my sketchbook and pencils and sat on the bed.

Drawing is my favourite thing. Ever since I can remember, I've been drawing. Some of my teachers get mad at me for doodling in the margins of my books, or on my hands if I don't have a book. They don't believe me when I tell them I can't help it, but it's true. If there's a pencil or a pen within range, I have to pick it up and draw.

I sketched Sophia Fane in her beautiful white dress. Then I drew her father, with his angry red face. I drew Polly and George and the fat cook and evil Mrs Hardwick. My favourite person to draw was Charles Ellerdale, with his vast stomach like a balloon at full stretch.

I didn't draw Alice. I was too disturbed by that look of hatred she'd given me.

I didn't have a meal and Anna didn't offer me one when she came home. When I got hungry, I just ate one of the many snacks I'd bought.

As day turned to evening, I started to get really

nervous. My stomach churned whenever I thought about midnight.

Nobody was making me do this, I reminded myself. I didn't have to go through with it. I could have asked Anna to swap rooms, and then we'd have both slept normally.

But for some crazy reason I actually wanted to go back in time again. Now that I knew that when I went to sleep in the past, I would wake up back in the present, it felt quite safe. I could go back to the past every night. And, to be honest, that would be a lot more fun than hanging around here dying of boredom for another three days. I could live in the past at night and just sleep through the tedious silent days in Anna's flat.

So if I wanted to go back in time again, there was nothing else for it. I would have to stay in my room until the second clock struck midnight.

I would have to face the ghost.

It happened exactly the same as it had happened the previous night. I had thought I'd be prepared this time, but the howling in the chimney was just as terrifying as it had been before, and the tapping on the windowpane still stopped my heart. But at least I knew now what would be waiting for me when I looked out of the window.

I pulled the curtains aside. And there was Sophia Fane, with that wild, haunted look in those eyes that stared straight into mine.

The second clock began to strike. Sophia raised

her hand and beckoned to me.

"Help me," she mouthed.

I felt sick with terror but I forced myself to extend my hand towards hers. I placed my palm flat against the windowpane. Sophia's hand didn't move, but she continued to look intently at me.

"I will help you," I said. "I promise. I will come into your time, and I will find a way for you and your baby to stay together. I promise."

Sophia continued to look into my eyes. I peeled my hand from the cold glass pane and walked towards the bedroom door. My heart was beating so hard it hurt.

As I passed through the doorway, I felt the same strange dissolving sensation I had felt the previous night. And as the door closed behind me, I felt myself becoming whole again. I was wearing the same clothes I had worn last night, with the corset tight around my ribcage and the itchy woollen stockings on my legs. And I was back in Sophia Fane's house, with its carved doors and blue walls and patterned rug, and the polished floorboards gleaming in the light of the wall lamps.

My heart was beating with excitement now, not fear. I really could travel through time! I could come here every night!

Suddenly I had a thought that filled me with panic. I would only be in Anna's flat for three more days. So I only had three days to help Sophia escape from her father and keep her baby.

Or did I? Because I didn't even know how the

time travel worked yet. Would time in the past have moved on, or would tonight be a repeat of last night?

I knew only one thing for certain. Sophia Fane was imprisoned on 27th April 1814. So the first thing I needed to do was to find out the date. And that shouldn't be too difficult, surely.

I was about to head downstairs when I realised I'd forgotten to bring the washing-up gloves and the chocolates. If I went back into my bedroom, would my things be there?

Slowly and carefully, I turned the shining brass knob and opened the door a few centimetres.

Somebody was breathing softly in the darkness. If this really was Sophia's room, then presumably that was her, asleep in bed. I couldn't see the bed from here and I didn't dare open the door any wider in case I woke her.

Long curtains were drawn across the window. I could make out a fireplace where, in my time, the wind howled in the chimney behind a blank wall. There was a carpet on the floor and a lot of heavy-looking furniture. The walls were covered with framed pictures.

None of my stuff was here. Everything was completely different. So I probably couldn't have brought the gloves and chocolates anyway. After all, I hadn't even got my own clothes on. It didn't seem as though anything at all could travel between the two worlds.

Apart from me.

PART TWO

CHAPTER TEN

Second Housemaid

Light streamed in from the high windows on the staircase. Birds were singing outside. It must be morning.

As I reached the stone-flagged passage that led to the kitchen, I heard footsteps on the stairs above me. I turned to see Polly. Her eyes widened in surprise.

"There you are," she said. "Where have you been? I thought you'd scarpered in the night."

"Er... I woke up early," I said.

"Oh, that happened to me too, my first morning. Give it a few days and you'll be snatching every minute of sleep you can get."

By the back door a man was buttoning his jacket. A narrow camp bed lay across the doorway.

"This is where George sleeps," said Polly. "William sleeps across the front door and he sleeps across the back."

George? Surely not the same George I met last night? This man had short dark hair and wore a plain brown jacket. He laughed as he saw me staring at him.

"Don't recognise me without the wig and livery, do you?"

"You look completely different," I said. "Why do you sleep across the back door? To stop burglars?"

"That's right." He folded the camp bed away and picked up something from underneath it. I stared.

"Is that a gun?"

"That's right. Musket."

"Do you always sleep with a gun under the bed?"

He packed the blankets and the gun into a high cupboard on the wall. "To be sure I do. Master's orders."

"Have you ever had a burglary?"

"Not in my time. But there was one a few years back. William and the other footman – John, it was then – they caught the men and locked them in the pantry. Sir Henry had them up before the judge."

"What happened to them?"

George slid open the top bolt on the back door. "Hanged, all three of them. Brothers, they was, the youngest barely twelve years old."

I gaped at him. "Hanged? A twelve-year-old?"

"Here you are, Evie," said Polly. She handed me a wooden box full of brushes, and a metal bucket containing sticks and a rough piece of cloth. She brought out a broom and a similar box for herself. Then she led me back to the room where the party was held last night. It was very dark now, with heavy wooden shutters across the windows. Last night's smells lingered faintly, like ghostly reminders.

Polly set her box down by the fireplace, so I did the same.

"You're second housemaid," she said, "so you're on fires. I do dusting, curtains and carpets."

She walked to one of the enormous windows and lifted the iron bar that held the shutters in place. She folded the shutters back and the room was filled with light. I looked at the clock on the mantelpiece. Half past five! No wonder the house was quiet.

"Polly," I asked, "what date is it today?"

"The twenty-fifth of April."

The twenty-fifth of April. The same date as it was in the present.

"And…" This was going to sound unbelievably stupid. But I had to find out. "And what year is it?"

Polly's eyebrows shot up. "Do you really not know what year it is?"

I shook my head. Clearly I was going to have to get used to being the village idiot.

"It's eighteen fourteen, you daft ha'porth," she said.

The twenty-fifth of April 1814.

In two days' time Sophia would be locked in her room for the rest of her life.

Unless I could do something to prevent it.

"Stir yourself, Evie," said Polly. "You need to get on with that fire."

I looked at the huge stone fireplace. The grate was filled with crumbly grey ash and the charred remains of logs. What was I supposed to do?

There was a fireplace in our flat in London but we

never had a fire. The grate was filled with pine cones I'd collected in the park.

"Could you show me, Polly?" I asked. "I've never made a fire before."

Polly gaped. "Never done a fire?"

"Well, not like this," I said hastily. "Ours was different. This is much ... grander."

"Right," she said in a businesslike manner. "First you roll up the hearthrug, so it's out of the way, and then you lay down your cloth to keep the place clean. Then you rake out the ashes like this, see."

She took an iron tool from a set hanging by the fire and clattered it to and fro across the bars of the grate, so that the ashes fell into the hearth.

"Leave the bigger cinders – you can use them to help start the fire. Now, take your kindling out of the bucket and lay it on the hearth there, then sweep out the ashes and put them in the bucket. Now you brush over all the fireplace with this," she said, taking a short-handled brush from the box. "Then you clean the bars and the fire-irons, first with this oil" – pulling a glass bottle from the box – "rubbed in with this cloth, and then rub them all down with emery paper." She took out a piece of grey sandpaper. "Then you do them all over with scouring paper. That's this one. Sir Henry's very fussy about clean fireplaces, so make sure you do it properly or you'll feel the back of Hardwitch's hand. Then you brush the back and sides of the fireplace with blacklead, and rub them dry with this brush here." She took yet another brush from the box, this one with hard-looking bristles.

My head was spinning. How many stages of fire-cleaning could there be?

Polly sat back on her heels. "Got that? When it's all done, you lay and light the fire. You've got your tinderbox there. Now, I must get on with the carpets or Hardwitch'll have my guts for garters."

I stared at the array of brushes and polishes and papers and cloths. How on earth would I remember all that?

Maybe if I put all the objects in the order I was meant to use them?

Once I had ordered everything, I called Polly across to check it. With a lot of tutting, she rearranged the line. "Come on, slowcoach," she said. "There's eight more fires to do before breakfast."

My jaw dropped. "You are kidding, right?"

Polly looked puzzled. "Come again?"

"I have to do eight more fireplaces? Before breakfast? No way!"

Polly stared at me. "What did you think? That a house this size has only one fire?" She looked at me as though she was trying to work me out. "You are a funny one." She got down on her hands and knees and started to sweep the huge rug with a little dustpan and brush. I rattled the iron poker along the bars of the grate to clear the ashes. Dust flew up all around me.

"Not like that, girl," said a harsh voice.

Mrs Hardwick was bustling across the room

towards me, and she was clearly in a filthy mood. "You're stirring up dust all over the room. Do it gently, for goodness' sake."

She lifted her hand and, unbelievably, smacked me on the side of the head again. Before I could even react, she whacked Polly across the side of her head too. "As for you," she said, "you've barely started your work. Out of bed late, were you?"

I jumped to my feet. "Hey! Don't hit Polly! She's only behind because she's showing me how to do things. You can't go around hitting people like that. It's against the law, you know. I'll report you!"

Her face turned crimson with fury and she hit me again.

"You mind your tongue, madam, or you'll get it twice as hard next time." She turned to go, muttering, "Hiring a girl from London, indeed. I don't know what they were thinking. Imbeciles, every one of them. And impudent little monkeys with it."

She swept out of the room, her keys rattling on their chain. My head throbbed and I was seething with fury.

"How dare she?" I said to Polly. "That's child abuse. I wish I'd hit her back."

To my amazement, Polly burst out laughing. She laughed so hard she almost fell over.

"Why are you laughing? She just hit you! What's funny about that?"

"You, that's what's funny," Polly spluttered. "Acting all high and mighty, like you'd never been touched before." She put on what was obviously meant to be an imitation of my voice. "You can't go around hitting people. I'll report you!" She burst into giggles again.

I stared at her. Clearly it was perfectly normal for people to hit children in this world.

Polly stopped laughing and looked at me curiously. "Have you really never been walloped?"

"Never," I said truthfully.

"Really?" She looked as though she wasn't sure whether to believe me. "Well, you're going to have to get used to it. Hardwitch is pretty free with her right arm, as you may have noticed. Now, set to on that fire, for goodness' sake, or we'll get another whacking."

I got down on my knees in front of the fire and picked up the first brush. To be honest, this servant stuff didn't look as though it was going to be much fun. Polly was really nice, but I didn't fancy many more hours on my hands and knees scrubbing fireplaces. Presumably Sophia was already engaged to the gardener. I just needed to find her and warn her about what her father was planning to do, so she could escape with her fiancé as soon as possible and I wouldn't have to come back here again.

"Polly," I said, as I rubbed the bars with oil, "have you ever noticed Sophia – I mean Miss Fane – with anybody else?"

Polly was on her hands and knees, combing the fringe of the rug perfectly straight.

"What do you mean?" she said.

"Does she seem to be in love with anyone? One of

77

the gardeners, for instance?"

Polly looked incredulous. "One of the gardeners? Are you mad? Ladies like Miss Fane don't fall in love with gardeners."

"No," I said. "Of course not."

"Get a move on, Evie, or we'll never be done."

The grit from the sandpaper got into my cuts, and they stung so badly that I had to bite my lip to stop myself from crying with the pain. By the time I'd finished, the fireplace gleamed.

"That looks lovely," said Polly.

"Who cares?" I said. "What's the point of a gleaming fireplace? It'll only get dirty again."

"Sir Henry likes everything spotless when he comes down in the morning," said Polly.

"Oh, well then, we must make everything spotless," I said sarcastically, "if that's what Sir Henry likes. Never mind that my hands are torn to shreds."

"Go on and make the fire then," said Polly. My sarcasm was wasted on her too.

I'd seen Nisha's mum lay a fire, so I knew how to make a grid with the little sticks and place small lumps of coal on top of them. Then I just had to light it.

I opened the tinderbox. It contained a short length of rough metal, a sharp flint, a few small squares of cotton and some thin splinters of wood that I guessed were matches. I struck one against the metal. Nothing happened.

I struck it against the flint. Nothing.

I tried another match. Nothing.

"Sorry, Polly, but I can't get these matches to light."

Polly straightened up, walked to the fireplace and took the flint, the piece of metal and a square of cloth. She laid the cloth on the hearth and, crouching over it, struck the metal against the flint. Sparks flew from the flint. After a few goes, one of them landed on the cloth. It started to smoulder, and a tiny flame appeared. Polly took one of the wood splinters and held it to the flame. Then she held the lighted splinter to a piece of kindling on the fire. She blew gently on the glowing wood and it started to flame up.

She sat back on her heels. "Now you're supposed to polish the coal scuttle and the hearth, but seeing as it's your first day, I'll do the scuttle for you, or we'll never get finished."

"Have you finished your cleaning?" I asked. Much as I would have loved her help, I didn't want to get her into any more trouble.

"I'm done in here," she said, kneeling down and unscrewing the lid of yet another pot of cleaning paste. "Once we've left, the footmen come in and clean the furniture and ornaments and looking glasses."

"They have two separate sets of people to clean a room? Why don't we just do it all? Not that I'm complaining," I added hastily.

"Us girls can't be trusted with the delicate things," said Polly. "That's a man's job. Girls just do the drudge's work. Like you scrubbing out them pans last night, while the footmen wash the china and glass."

"But that's so unfair!" I said. "Washing china and glass is way easier than scrubbing out pans with sand."

Polly shrugged. "It's just how it is."

I made a mental note to check out the footmen's hands. I bet they weren't cut to shreds, I thought, if all they had to do was dust the ornaments and rinse out a few glasses.

Once the scuttle and hearth were shining, Polly got to her feet and grinned at me.

"There you are. Just four more fires on this floor and then we go up and do the dressing rooms."

"I can't do eight more of these," I said. "It's impossible."

Polly sighed. "Tell you what, I'll rush about with the cleaning and then I should have time to do a couple of the fires. But only today, mind."

"You're so kind, Polly," I said, hugging her. "Thank you so much."

She looked startled, but quite pleased.

"To tell the truth," she said, "it's nice to have a bit of company. It's a terrible lonely job when you have to do it by yourself." She opened the door and led the way across the hall, indicating a door on the far side. "Right, I'll sweep the hall here while you do the fire in the White Parlour."

CHAPTER ELEVEN

The Boy Outside
the Window

In the White Parlour the shutters were already open. I drew back the heavy curtains of the window nearest to the fireplace. Outside, a beautiful green lawn sloped down to a thick hedge. In the slanting early morning sunlight, birds hopped about on the grass and sang in the trees. It was incredibly quiet and peaceful, and I could have stood there for ages, drinking it all in, but I could hear Polly clattering about in the next room. If I didn't get a move on, then poor Polly would have even more to do. So I set my box down by the fireplace, knelt on my aching knees and started to rake out the ashes, more gently this time, since I didn't especially fancy another smack around the head.

I was rubbing the fire tools with emery paper, thinking I would willingly swap everything I owned for that pair of rubber gloves, when, from right behind me, there came the most enormous sneeze.

I shrieked and leapt to my feet, dropping the poker in the hearth with a massive clang.

Peeping out from between the closed curtains at

the other window was Sophia Fane. Her eyes were huge and terrified.

I stared at her. "Have you been there the whole time?"

Sophia pressed her finger to her lips. "Sshh."

"Sorry," I whispered. "You gave me a shock, that's all. I didn't think anyone was here."

Sophia stood completely still. She seemed to be listening intently for something. I listened too, wondering what she was afraid of. The only sounds I could hear were birdsong and Polly's rhythmic sweeping in the next room.

Slowly, Sophia removed her finger from her lips. She stepped forward, frowning slightly as she looked at me.

"You are new," she said eventually, in a low voice. "What is your name?"

"Evie," I replied, and then remembered to add, "Miss Fane."

She looked at me curiously. "You don't look like a housemaid," she said.

"No," I said. It was on the tip of my tongue to say that I had actually come from the future to help her. But, just in time, I thought about how that would sound. If she thought I was a lunatic, she would never take my warning seriously.

So instead I said, "You're up very early."

Sophia's cheeks flushed. "I... I rose early to read. You must not mention it to a soul. If my father were to find out, he would be furious."

I laughed. It seemed so ridiculous that anyone

could get in trouble for getting up early to read a book.

"Be quiet," hissed Sophia, flapping her hands urgently. "I am serious. My father was so angry that I was reading during the ball last night that he has banned me from reading entirely. So you will make no mention of this."

She said that last sentence like somebody who was used to giving orders. And I remembered her father's fury when he had seen her reading at the ball.

"I won't breathe a word," I said.

"And especially not to Madame Perrault."

"Who's Madame Perrault?"

"She was my governess, until I grew too old for such a thing. And anyway," she said with a bitter little laugh, "what use would a governess be, now that I am no longer permitted to read? Now she is called my lady's maid, although she is really a spy. She reports me to my father for the slightest little thing. Her only redeeming feature is that, since she is so old, she sleeps a lot. Hence my habit of rising early."

"I won't say a word, I promise. You can trust me."

She nodded. "Well, continue with your work."

I found this a bit offensive but I stopped myself from answering back. I decided to work out how to deliver my warning as I carried on doing the fire.

And then, as Sophia parted the curtains, I glimpsed something outside the window.

Or, rather, some*one*.

Of course! How could I have believed that rubbish

about her coming down early to read? If she wanted to read, why would she come downstairs and risk being caught, when she could just read in bed?

"Let me open these curtains for you," I said.

"Oh, no … I…"

I drew the curtains open.

Under a tree on the other side of the path, his back against the trunk, sat a boy of I would guess about eighteen. He wore a black hat, a brown jacket and brown trousers. He had a board balanced on his knees, with a sheet of paper on it, and he was drawing something with a quill pen. A bottle of ink stood at his side.

Sophia's eyes were fixed on her book. As if she could fool me like that. Her cheeks were bright red.

"Thank you," she said, without looking up from the book, and her tone had a finality about it that clearly said: *Go back to work.*

I returned to the fireplace and began to oil the bars. That boy must be the gardener she's secretly engaged to, I thought.

Still oiling the bars, I stole a glance at Sophia. The book lay open on her lap as she looked out of the window. The corners of her mouth twitched in a little smile.

Furtively, I pushed my box away from me until it was close to the other window. Not that I really needed to be furtive. Sophia was in another world.

Under the guise of fetching a brush from the box, I stood up and glanced out of the window. The boy had finished his drawing and he held it up for Sophia to see.

He was seriously good at art. His drawing was a perfect caricature of Mrs Hardwick, accentuating all her bony angles. Somehow he had even caught her furious, bustling energy.

Sophia laughed. Then she clapped a hand over her mouth and glanced across to me. I grabbed the nearest brush, knelt down on the hearth and brushed the back and sides of the fireplace with blacklead. I laid the fire and tried to light it, but I couldn't coax a spark to light the tinder. I would have to fetch Polly. But first I needed to deliver my warning to Sophia, while we were alone together.

I pulled myself upright, my back aching. This was how it must feel to be old.

Now both the boy outside the window and Sophia, on the windowseat, were drawing in sketchbooks. I wondered how they had met, and whether it was their love of art that had brought them together.

I slipped to the edge of the bay window, so that the boy wouldn't see me if he glanced up again. From where I was standing, I could see Sophia's drawing over her shoulder.

I almost laughed out loud. It was a caricature of Charles Ellerdale, and it captured perfectly the straining waistcoat buttons over his enormous paunch, the bulging toad-like eyes and that arrogant way he stood as though he was the most important person in the room. I watched in admiration as Sophia's pen flew over the paper. I knew she'd be furious if she caught me looking, but she seemed to have forgotten I was there.

When she finished, she held the sketchbook up to the window and tapped gently on the glass.

I drew back to avoid being seen. But I bumped into a piece of furniture behind me. Something rattled, and Sophia whipped her head round, grabbed her sketchbook and jumped up, glaring at me.

"What are you doing?" she snapped, her face scarlet. "How dare you spy on me?"

"I'm not spying. I was just walking past. I've got to fetch Polly to help me light the fire. I won't say anything to anyone, I promise."

Sophia started to sweep up her things from the windowseat into her arms. I needed to warn her quickly. I might not have another chance to be alone with her today. And I couldn't bear the thought of another day working as a housemaid.

"Miss Fane," I said, bobbing a little curtsey for extra effect, "I have to warn you of something."

She turned to me, her sketchbook and pencils clutched in her arms, her expression a mixture of anger and fear.

"Er, Miss Fane," I stumbled, wishing I had thought more about how I was going to say this, "has your father said anything to you about who he wants you to marry?"

Sophia looked briefly bewildered as well as furious and terrified. Then she drew herself up very tall and took a step towards me. I could tell she was about to throw me out of the room, so I jumped in before she had the chance.

"Sorry for being rude, and I know you don't know me or anything," I gabbled, "but it's just that I happen to know he's going to try and make you marry Mr Ellerdale, and if you don't want to do that, you and that boy should run away together now, or— *Ow*! Stop it!"

I stared at Sophia, my eyes smarting from the slap she had just given me.

"How *dare* you speak to me like this?" she hissed. She looked almost mad with emotion. "Get out of my sight! Do not speak to me ever again. And if you breathe one word of this nonsense to another living soul, I shall have you whipped, do you understand me?"

She was advancing on me as she spoke, until I was trapped, backed up against the door. Then she shoved me out of the way, pulled the door open and swept out of the room.

Well.

What had I done to deserve this? Wasn't it bad enough that I'd been forced to go and stay with a crazy, skeleton-loving old woman who didn't even own a TV, without then being whisked back two hundred years in time? I mean, who goes back in time?

It wouldn't have been so bad if I was one of those rich people at the party last night, but oh no, I end up on my hands and knees scrubbing out fireplaces. It was like some kind of giant cosmic joke. And what had I ever done to the universe?

And then when I tried to do a good thing and

warn Sophia that she was about to be locked up for the rest of her life, what thanks did I get? A slap in the face and the threat of being whipped. Nice.

Well, if she was going to treat me like that, I thought, let her be locked up forever. She actually deserves it.

CHAPTER TWELVE

Alice

Finished! I laid the final piece of kindling on my final fire of the morning. Every bone in my body ached. Muscles ached in places where I didn't even know I had muscles.

Now, I thought, let's see if I can manage to light this one myself.

I took out my tinderbox, laid the square of cloth on the hearth and, without hope, struck the flint against the steel. Sparks shot out and, to my astonishment, one of them landed on the tinder and began to smoulder.

"It's caught!" I called to Polly, who was dusting the dressing-table.

"Quick," she said, "put a match to it."

I held one of the wood splinters (they were dipped in sulphur, Polly told me) against the smouldering tinder. To my delight, a little flame appeared at the tip of the match. I inched it towards the fire and held it to the thinnest piece of kindling. A splinter began to glow orange.

"Oh, go on, go on," I murmured, crouching over the tiny flame.

The splinter curled up and turned black. I blew gently on it, as I'd seen Polly do, but it remained resolutely black. I sat back on my haunches and sighed.

"Sorry, Polly. Failed again."

"It's a good job it's not Tuesday," said Polly as she crossed the room. "That's carpet-cleaning day."

"But you've cleaned the carpets today."

"No, today's just sweeping. On Tuesdays we have to sprinkle damp tea leaves on them and sweep them off."

"Tea leaves?"

"They attract the dust, that's the idea. Once a month we do it with damp salt, and you should see how black the salt gets. Salt works better, I reckon. But salt costs, and the tea leaves have already been used, so they'd only go to feed the pigs."

We were in Sophia's dressing room, which was now Anna's bedroom. It was such a weird thought that here I was, working as a housemaid in the exact same place where, two hundred years in the future, my godmother was asleep in bed.

"Right," said Polly, "that's done. Now for water."

"Oh, yes, please," I said, suddenly realising how thirsty I was.

Polly gave me a funny look. "You *like* carrying water?"

"Carrying water? What do you mean? Why do we have to carry water?"

"So the family can wash, of course. You must have had servants carrying water for you, surely, before

90

you came down in the world?"

"Oh. Yes, of course."

"You take that bowl." She indicated a marble-topped table on which stood a huge china bowl and matching jug. The bowl was half full of water, with a film of soap scum floating on the top.

"I'll fetch Sir Henry's," Polly said. "We empty them in the scullery sink and clean them out."

"Imagine," I said, as we carried the heavy bowls downstairs, "if the water could be carried around the house in pipes, and you could just turn on a tap and it would pour out."

"Carried around the house in pipes?" said Polly. "What are you talking about?"

"Never mind. Just thinking aloud."

What was I doing, carrying Sophia Fane's dirty washing water down three flights of stairs? It was madness. But the time travel only seemed to happen at night. So I was going to have to put up with being a servant for the rest of the day. Great.

We walked through an enormously long brick cellar, lined on both sides with hundreds of wooden barrels.

"The beer cellar," Polly explained.

"Wow. You people drink a lot of beer."

We carried the bowls along a corridor, past a series of rooms that Polly named as the servants' hall, the dairy, the game larder and the pantry. As we passed, she said hello to a maid working in the dairy. I was curious to see what she was doing, but Polly hurried along too fast for me to stop.

As we got to the scullery where I washed up last night, Alice emerged from the kitchen with a pile of dirty pans. The cook's voice shouted from behind her. "And then get straight back here and peel those carrots, you useless little slattern."

Alice gave me a look of loathing as she walked into the scullery, where a little girl was washing up at the sink. She was so small that she had to stand on a wooden box. She must be Nell, the scullery maid who fainted last night, I thought. If only I had those rubber gloves to give her.

Alice dumped the pans on the draining board. She stepped back for Polly to enter the scullery, but she didn't wait for me to go in. Instead, she walked out and shoved me in the elbow, sending the greasy water in my bowl slopping on to the floor.

"Hey!" I said. "What did you do that for?"

"Clumsy idiot," she said, a malicious gleam in her eye. "What a mess you've made."

She walked back into the kitchen and shut the door behind her.

Polly came out of the scullery. Her serene expression turned to a frown as she saw the puddle on the floor and streams of water flowing down the channels between the flagstones.

"Oh, Evie," she said. "How did you manage to do that?"

"I didn't. Alice shoved me, on purpose. She hates me. She's hated me from the first moment she saw me."

Polly said nothing. She fetched two cloths from

the scullery and handed one to me.

"Why does she hate me?" I said, as I mopped up the water. "I haven't done anything to her."

Polly got down on her hands and knees and started mopping.

"She's jealous," she said.

"Of me? Why?"

Polly laughed. "Beats me. You can't even light a fire."

I couldn't help laughing too. It was hard to feel miserable with Polly around.

"She hates being a kitchen maid," said Polly.

"But why would that make her hate me?"

"Because she wanted your job."

"She *wanted* this job? Why's it better than being a kitchen maid?"

"Imagine being stuck in that kitchen working for that nasty old cook all day long. Old Winter loathes all kitchen maids. She makes their lives a misery."

"I don't see this is much better," I said. "I've already been hit three times by Mrs Hardwick."

"At least she's not breathing over our shoulders all day long though," said Polly. "Mostly we get to work by ourselves. And Alice wanted to work with me, of course. Who wouldn't?" She grinned at me. "But Alice can't sew, and you have to be able to sew to be a housemaid. I was lucky that way. We was all taught to sew, where I grew up."

"Did you grow up near here?" I asked, wringing my cloth into the bowl.

"Over on the edge of the village," said Polly. "In the workhouse."

"Oh."

We'd learned about workhouses in history, when we did the Victorians, and, from what I remember, they were cruel, horrible places, the absolute last resort for people who had nowhere else to go.

I mopped up water from between the flagstones. "So are you ... an orphan?"

"I don't know. My mother died when I was a baby, so they told me. They found me on the workhouse steps one morning. They reckoned my father took me there and then left the village. Probably went off to find work."

"He abandoned you? That's terrible."

Polly shrugged. "Happens to a lot of people. Times is hard, with that dratted war."

War? Was England at war in 1814? I almost asked which war, but stopped myself just in time. I didn't want Polly to think I was even more stupid than she thought I was already.

"At least he took me to the workhouse," she said. "So he must have cared about me. Else he'd have just left me to die. And here I am, alive and well."

"How long have you been working here?"

"About two years now. I was hired out to the silk factory, but it was terrible work and somebody told me about a girl what worked here. So I ran away one day and just turned up here. I said I was a hard worker and good at sewing and old Hardwitch agreed to try me out. I was lucky – they'd just had a maid leave, so they needed another pair of hands. She's a tough old boot, Hardwitch, but she's got a decent heart. It's buried pretty deep, but it's there." She stood up. "All done. Get rid of that water and give your hands a wash, now the fires are done."

I tipped the dirty water down the sink that Nell wasn't using, and then Polly put the plug in. I said hello to Nell, and she gave me a frightened glance in reply. She only looked about ten, poor thing.

While Polly sloshed water into the sink from a bucket, I opened the kitchen door very slightly and peeped through. It looked much more cheerful in daylight. Mrs Winter waddled to the oven, stooped down and took out a big tray of perfect bread rolls. She might be evil but she could clearly cook. The smell of fresh bread made my mouth water. My stomach felt hollow from hunger.

"Come on, Evie," said Polly. "Hurry up and wash your hands."

I took the bar of soap and plunged my hands into the cold water. Polly held out a scrubbing brush.

I recoiled in horror. "Are you *mad*? It's bad enough putting soap on these cuts. How do you stand it?"

Polly smiled sympathetically. "It's terrible at first. But the skin toughens up after a while."

"Why don't you wear gloves?"

"We had a girl last year tried that. Bought a pair of leather gloves and they were ruined in a few days. I'm not about to spend my earnings on leather gloves to watch them getting wrecked. Better to grow a thicker skin, I reckon, don't you, Nell?"

Nell gave her a nervous little smile.

So rubber gloves hadn't been invented in 1814. I imagined how out of place my bright-yellow washing-up gloves would have looked in this world.

"Poor Nell was in dreadful pain with her hands when she started," said Polly, "but they're better now, aren't they, Nell?"

She ruffled Nell's hair with her work-worn hands. "Right," she said. "Let's clean these bowls out and take them back upstairs."

I'd never thought before about what it would be like to live in a house with no running water. Well, I can tell you now, it's a nightmare.

After we'd done the washstand bowls, we had to fill massive metal watering cans with hot water from the copper and take them to the dressing rooms. Stupidly, I filled my cans far too full, so the hot water kept slopping over the top and scalding me. I had to set them down and rest every few steps and my back and hands hurt worse than ever by the time I finished.

I met Polly on the landing as I came out of Sir Henry's dressing room. "Ready for breakfast?" she said.

I looked at her warily. "Eating it, or taking it to other people?"

Polly laughed. "Eating it, of course."

"Oh, yes, please, I'm starving."

As soon as the words were out of my mouth, I wished I could take them back. Polly was so thin that her bones jutted through her skin, but she hadn't complained once.

Polly led the way back downstairs. The clock on the first-floor landing showed half past eight.

Only half past eight! I'd already done more housework that morning than in the rest of my life put together. By rights, I should have still been in bed. If I had to work this hard all day, I'd probably be dead by evening.

CHAPTER THIRTEEN

Breakfast

"We have our meals in the servants' hall," said Polly as we walked through the beer cellar.

It wasn't really a hall, more like a very plain dining room. There was a fireplace at one end, but no fire in it. The only furniture was a long wooden table, laid with plates and knives, with benches down both sides and a chair at each end. In the middle of the table sat a solid-looking loaf of bread on a board and a dish of butter.

George and another man walked in, talking, and sat on one of the benches. They wore brown leather aprons over their jackets.

"William, this is Evie, the new housemaid," said Polly. "William's the other footman, Evie."

I said hello. The men nodded and continued their conversation – something to do with a horse that Sir Henry was thinking of buying. William was as tall as George, and looked about the same age, but thinner and paler, with dark hair.

Polly and I sat down on the other bench. Suddenly I had a thought. Perhaps the gardeners had their breakfast in here. If Sophia wasn't going to listen to me, then maybe I could talk to the gardener she was in love with instead. After all, he was a servant too. Surely he wouldn't hit me if I tried to speak to him.

I was about to ask Polly when the door at the other end of the room opened and two girls walked in, giggling. They were older than me and Polly – fifteen or sixteen maybe. One was tall and skinny, with dark hair and eyes, and the other was shorter and curvier, with a freckled face and curly red hair showing under her cap. This was the girl I had seen working in the dairy earlier. They sat opposite us and looked at me curiously.

"This is Evie, the new housemaid," said Polly. "She's come from London."

"Pleased to meet you, Evie," said the red-haired girl.

"Hello," I said.

"Evie, this is Betty," said Polly, indicating the red-haired one. "She's the dairymaid. She's in love with Dan Greenwood, the farmer's son over at Home Farm."

"Polly!" exclaimed Betty. "What a thing to say!" But she looked pleased.

"And this is Mary, the laundry maid," said Polly, pointing to the dark-haired girl.

"And she's not in love with anybody," said Mary.

"Mary pleases herself," added Betty, and Mary giggled. Her hands looked even redder and sorer than mine.

"Set to with that loaf, will you, George," said

Mary. "I'm crust-hungry, I am."

George started sawing slices off the dense loaf.

"Will the gardeners be coming to breakfast?" I asked Polly in a low voice. The others were talking, so I didn't think they'd hear me, but Mary's ears pricked up.

"Oh, interested in the gardeners, is she?"

Betty groaned. "You're not sweet on Robbie, are you, Evie?"

"Everybody's sweet on Robbie," said Mary.

"Except Alice," said Betty, "who prefers Jacob, for some mysterious reason."

"Who's Robbie?" I asked.

"See, Evie doesn't even know who Robbie is," said Polly, "so give over with your teasing." She turned to me. "Robbie's the under-gardener. *Some* people," she said, raising her eyebrows at Mary, "think he's very handsome."

"Does he have wavy brown hair?" I asked. "And wear a black hat?"

Polly looked surprised. "How do you know that?"

"I saw him from the window of the White Parlour when I was making the fire. So do they have their breakfast in here?"

"No, the gardeners eat at the farmhouse," said Betty. "So you won't be able to feast your eyes on Robbie over the breakfast table."

Well, at least I knew his name now. That felt like progress, of a sort. And I could try to find him in the garden, if I was ever able to leave the house.

"Don't go falling in love with him," said Mary.

"They say he already has a sweetheart. Not that we've ever seen her."

"How was the ball, George?" asked Betty. "Was the master pleased with it?"

"Hard to tell," said George, passing slices of bread around. "He was none the better for what he'd took, but nothing new about that. Miss Fane didn't half get it once the guests had left."

"Poor thing," said Betty. "I never see her no more."

"He's banned her from coming down here, that's why," said George. "She mustn't pick up common habits from the servants. Wants her to be a lady now she's about to get married."

Mary shuddered. "To that fat old piece of blubber?"

"Rich old piece of blubber, mind you," said George. "Lovely butter today, Betty. Better than that rotten old stuff you made on Thursday."

"Oi, you cheeky beggar," said Betty. "You watch it or you'll get none tomorrow."

I was so hungry by now that anything would have tasted good, and that bread and butter tasted better than any meal I'd ever eaten.

"I wouldn't have old Ellerdale if he was rich as the king himself," said Mary through a mouthful of bread.

"I would," said Polly. "I'd live like a queen and never scrub a floor again. I'd have hands as soft as silk and I'd be as fat as an empress. And I'd wear satin and lace from my head to my toes."

William gave Polly a serious look. "It wouldn't be

worth any amount of riches to be shackled to that man," he said. "He's a nasty piece of work. I heard he beat his last wife something terrible."

"He beat his wife?" I exclaimed. "And Sir Henry still wants his daughter to marry him?"

George snorted. "Sir Henry wouldn't worry about that. He's pretty free with his fists himself."

"But if Miss Fane won't have him, what will happen to us?" said Mary. "The master won't be able to hold on to Charlbury much longer if Miss Fane doesn't make a good match."

"Maybe she'll find another rich man to marry," said Betty.

"Oh, yes," said George, "and how many wealthy widowers do you know hereabouts? The master's had this marriage planned for years. No, if Miss Fane refuses Ellerdale, we're all doomed. There's not a penny left in the master's coffers and, from what I hear, he has debts stacked up all over the county."

"She'll marry him in the end," said William. "The master will make sure of it."

The talk moved on to other topics, but I wasn't listening any more. Sophia's father was going to try to force her to marry a violent man, and if she refused, he was going to lock her up for the rest of her life. Somehow I had to warn her. She needed to run away, and she needed to go as soon as possible.

I became aware that a hush had fallen over the room. I looked up to see Mrs Hardwick, the huge bunch of keys dangling at her waist, seating herself in the empty chair at the head of the table. William handed her a slice of bread. Was that all we were going to get? Surely there'd be something to drink? I was desperate for a glass of water.

"How's your mother faring, William?" Mrs Hardwick asked in a surprisingly kind tone.

William pulled a face. "Not so good, missus. But we're hoping she'll pull through."

"And your brothers and sisters?"

His face brightened a little. "They're well, so I hear. They're all at the spinning factory in the village now."

"Even little Thomas?" asked Mrs Hardwick. "How old is he now?"

"Just turned four, missus. He's a good little worker, they say."

Alice appeared and set down a tray with a jug and several grey metal mugs on it. Thank goodness.

William poured the honey-coloured drinks and Alice handed them round, shooting me an evil look as she slammed mine in front of me. I took a big gulp and instantly spat it across the table.

"Ugh!" I spluttered. It was bitter and horrible, like nothing I'd ever tasted. Had Alice poisoned my drink?

Everybody was staring at me.

"Sorry," I muttered, wiping up the mess with my napkin.

"What is wrong with the beer, young lady?" asked Mrs Hardwick in an icy tone. "Are you used to better?"

Beer? For *breakfast*?

"It's just … I normally drink water," I said.

"You drink the *water*? In *London*?" said Mary.

"I expect she lived near a spring," said George. "There do be springs in London, some places."

Mrs Hardwick shuddered. "Nasty dirty place, London. I wouldn't touch a thing from there. The food's all poisoned."

"Drink up your beer," said William. "Give you strength, it will."

I took another sip. It was really horrible. But I was so thirsty I had to drink something. Then I remembered what Polly had said about tea leaves.

"Excuse me, Mrs Hardwick," I said in my politest tone. "Could I please have a cup of tea instead?"

The footmen stopped their conversation and gaped at me. The girls giggled. Mrs Hardwick pursed her lips very tight.

"I don't know what sort of household you're used to," she said, "but in this house, tea is for family use only. It is not to be consumed by servants."

"Mrs Hardwick," said George in a high voice, "this beer is not to my taste. Could I possibly have a glass of your finest champagne?"

Betty and Mary roared with laughter. Even serious-faced William smiled.

"Leave off, you lot," said Polly. "Evie's come down in the world. It's not her fault she's used to better things." She turned to me. "Take no notice, Evie. Eat your bread and butter. You've a long morning ahead of you."

"Keep a close eye on her, Polly," said Mrs

Hardwick, "and make it clear exactly how we do things in this house."

"Yes, Mrs Hardwick," said Polly. "I'll train her up in no time, don't you worry."

CHAPTER FOURTEEN

Coal Scuttles and Chamber Pots

The coal buckets banged against my legs as I heaved them up the stairs. They were so heavy that I had to keep stopping to rest.

"Hurry up," said Polly. "We won't half catch it if they see us."

"Who?"

Polly sighed with impatience and picked up my bucket as well as her own. "The gentlemen, of course. We're not supposed to be seen. It embarrasses them."

"Why?"

"They might feel they should offer to help. They're brought up to be polite to ladies. They don't like to be reminded it's ladies what carries their coals."

"What, so we're supposed to keep out of sight so as not to embarrass the lazy rich men we're waiting on?" I said.

Polly gave me a frightened glance. "You mustn't talk like that, Evie. It's them what pays our wages."

"Well, they should be reminded of what we do. Why should we be invisible?"

"Listen, Evie," said Polly, setting down the buckets at the top of the stairs and turning to face me. "You may be used to better things but you're a servant now, just like the rest of us, so you'd better forget these airs and graces and knuckle down to work if you want to keep your place."

I had no intention of keeping my place for longer than a day, but I liked Polly a lot and I didn't want to annoy her, so I nodded silently in a humble and servant-like manner and picked up my coal bucket again.

The coal had to be poured into copper scuttles and the scuttles polished with another gritty mixture that stung my hands and scoured them red-raw again. Then the fires had to be stoked up. I managed to put out the first fire I touched, by smothering it with coal.

"Oh, Evie," Polly sighed. "Look, you just do the scuttles, and I'll stoke the fires. Go and do the Great Parlour. I'll come in and do the fire once I've finished in here."

The Great Parlour – I remembered doing the fire in there earlier. I lugged my coal bucket downstairs.

The door to the Great Parlour stood ajar. The rattle of crockery and the smell of coffee drifting into the hall meant the family must be having their breakfast in there. I peeped around the doorframe.

At the table in the centre of the room sat Sophia, with her father, frowning over a newspaper, and Mrs Bailey, her aunt. George, now in the full splendour of his livery, stood as still as a statue at the side of the room.

The table was laid with a snowy-white cloth. On

the cloth sat coffee pots and teapots and a feast of cakes and breads that made my mouth water. So this was where those lovely rolls went.

"And Madame Perrault informs me," Mrs Bailey was saying to Sophia, "that your petticoat was simply *covered* in mud yesterday. And your boots, she says, were practically ruined."

"A few spots of mud was all," said Sophia. "I took a walk in the wood. The bluebells are so beautiful and their scent was so heavenly after the rain, and they last for such a short time that I couldn't bear to miss them."

Her aunt shook her head. "I simply cannot approve of this solitary walking and riding. I wonder that you indulge your daughter in such activities, Sir Henry. Surely it is not right that she should wander the country unchaperoned in this wild manner?"

Sophia's father didn't seem to have heard. He was too busy slurping coffee, stuffing toast in his mouth and muttering at the newspaper, which was enormous, and covered in columns and columns of tiny print, with not a single picture.

Sophia glared at her aunt. "I am already forbidden to read," she said. "You have banned me from speaking to the servants. Am I to be forbidden from walking in the grounds of my own house too?"

Sir Henry looked up from the newspaper. "More toast," he barked at George.

As George moved to the table, he noticed me lurking outside the door. He looked so shocked that I panicked and blundered into the room with my bucket. "Polly said to fill the scuttle," I blurted out.

There was a deathly silence. Mrs Bailey looked horrified. Sophia looked startled, then afraid. Did she think I was about to tell her father what I'd seen earlier?

Sir Henry glared at George. "What's the skivvy doing in here?" he growled.

George flapped his hands at me, hustling me from the room as though he was swatting a fly. I stumbled out, the bucket banging against my shin. I heaved it up the stairs and along the first floor corridors, until I found Polly, blowing at a fire.

"Why did you tell me to go to the Great Parlour?" I said. "They were having breakfast in there and I got shooed out as though I was a flea-ridden rodent. Was that your idea of a joke?"

"Oh!" said Polly. "You daft ha'porth, you didn't go to the Great Parlour, you went to the Great *Chamber*. Oh, dear, did you get in trouble?"

"Oh no," I said in my most sarcastic tone. "They were delighted to see me. Sir Henry called me a skivvy and his sister looked at me as if I was a nasty smell."

"She looks at all of us like that," said Polly. "Don't fret about it."

"How do you stand it?"

"Stand what?"

"Working so hard for people who look down on you like that?"

"You just have to get on with it," said Polly, "and not think about it too much. There's a lot of people far worse off."

Seeing the look of disbelief on my face, she said, "I know we're drudging all day, but at least we get paid for it. And we have our own beds. There was four of us in the bed at the workhouse. Crawling with bugs, it was. Though four bodies do warm the bed up. I've never been so cold as I was last winter. But I don't get beaten that much here. And we get fed too. I'll never forget my first meal in the servants' hall. When I saw meat on my plate my eyes nearly popped out of my head. I'd only smelled meat before, never tasted it. It was the best meal I'd ever had in my life. And when Mrs H asked if I'd like a second helping, well, my jaw nearly hit the floor. You was lucky to get a first helping in the workhouse. We thought it was only royalty got seconds."

"It must have been horrendous."

"It weren't much fun. I'm glad I had the guts to run away."

After we'd prepared all the living rooms, I wearily followed Polly back up to the bedroom floor.

"This is Mrs Bailey's bedchamber," said Polly, opening a door into a large, gloomy, stale-smelling room. "First you open the windows and turn back the bedclothes to air the bed."

She walked to the far window and I drew back the curtains of the nearer one.

"Oh!" I gasped.

I undid the catch, flung the window open and leaned my head out. Under a perfect blue sky was a bright-green lawn surrounded by tall trees just coming into leaf. Beyond the trees, I caught glimpses of flowerbeds and statues and bushes cut into shapes, and paths that led to archways in hedges, and painted wooden doors in curved brick walls, and a hundred other things I wanted to explore. And beyond the gardens lay fields and farmyards and woods and valleys and hills, stretching on and on until they faded to a soft blue in the far, far distance. And from far and near, high and low, the air was filled with layer upon layer upon layer of birdsong: chirruping, calling, singing, twittering and chirping.

Wait. Could that really be what it sounded like? I'd never heard one in real life.

"Polly," I said, "is that a cuckoo?"

Polly listened. The call came again. "Yes, that's him. That's the first I've heard this year. It's properly spring now then."

"They really do say 'Cuckoo'. That's amazing."

"Come and help me turn back the bedclothes," said Polly. "We'll never get everything done if you keep dawdling."

"Do we ever get the chance to go into the gardens?" I asked her.

"We get an hour off in the afternoon," Polly replied. "If the family aren't using the gardens, we're allowed to walk in the kitchen garden and the orchard. Not the formal gardens, mind. They're out of bounds to servants."

Of course they are, I thought. Heaven forbid that servants might pollute the grass.

Two men carrying garden tools emerged on to the lawn from a tree-lined path. The younger one, I was sure, was the boy who had been drawing with Sophia this morning.

"Is that Robbie?" I asked.

Polly sighed and walked across.

"Yes, that's him. With Mr Masters, the head gardener. Now, will you just come and help with these bedclothes."

As we wrestled with the surprisingly heavy bedclothes, I decided that I would make it my business to go and find Robbie during my hour off. I reckoned there was more chance of him listening to my warning than Sophia, and he might be able to talk some sense into her.

"Right," Polly said as we finished the bed. "Chamber pots next."

"What's a—" I began. Then I stopped as the memory came back. I looked warily at Polly. "What do you mean?"

"There's a chamber pot under every bed. You carry it down to the laundry – I'll show you – empty the slops, scour it out and bring it back."

"No *way* am I doing that!"

Polly laughed. "You didn't think they emptied their own slops, did you?"

"But that's disgusting! I'm not doing it. I can't. I'd be sick."

Polly's face tightened. "So you want me to empty them all?"

"No, of course not. I just…" I tailed off.

112

"Or you want them emptied by magic, is that it? Do you think some good fairy's going to come and do it for you?"

"No," I muttered. I wished I'd never said anything. Polly was the only friend I had in this world, and now she hated me too.

Polly sighed. "Look, I know you've come down in the world, Evie, and I know it must be a shock. You're used to having servants yourself, not serving somebody else. But you're a housemaid now, and that's what we do. So pick up the chamber pot, I'll go and get his lordship's and we'll take them down together."

I hated that she thought I was some awful spoiled brat. I wished I could tell her that I'd never had a servant and that my whole flat in London was smaller than this room. But if I told her that, then my uselessness as a servant would make no sense to her at all. So I meekly said, "OK. Sorry, Polly."

"OK?" she repeated. "What does that mean?"

"Oh, it's just a London word. It means 'all right'."

Taking a deep breath, I steeled myself to look under the bed.

Oh, thank goodness. Mrs Bailey's chamber pot had a lid. I'd never been so grateful for anything in my life. As we trudged downstairs again, I tried to pretend I was doing something perfectly ordinary which didn't disgust me at all. Polly opened a door at the foot of the stairs and at last we were outdoors in the sunshine.

We were standing on a gravel drive, facing a neat,

cobbled stable yard. A beautiful chestnut-brown horse looked out of a stable door. In the distance, chickens squawked and sheep baaed. In the centre of the yard was a well with a low wall around it and, over the well, a rope wound around a cylinder, with a handle at the side.

A boy who looked a few years older than me, with straggly blond hair and a sulky-looking face, appeared around the corner, carrying a bundle of hay. He looked at me curiously.

"Jacob," muttered Polly when we were out of earshot. "Stable boy. Bad-tempered so-and-so."

I glanced back at Jacob and found to my surprise that he was still staring at me. I turned away quickly. There was something in his expression that made me uncomfortable. I was glad to follow Polly into the building on the far side of the yard.

"This is the laundry," she said.

The laundry was a long, low building, warm from a coal fire in the corner. On one side of the fire was a big copper like the one in the kitchen. On the other side was a flat metal surface, with five black irons sitting on it. A vast stone sink with long wooden draining boards stood under the window. Washing was soaking in two huge wooden tubs on the stone floor.

From the yard came the sound of a girl's voice, singing. The door opened and Mary walked in, carrying an overflowing basket of muddy clothes. She broke off singing and smiled at us.

"Tip those in here, girls," she said, pointing to a

bucket in the corner of the laundry. "I'll be needing all I can get, with this lot to wash."

"What do you mean?" I asked.

Polly grinned. "The family don't get told this, but there's nothing better than a bit of stale pee for getting the dirt out of riding clothes."

Mary burst into laughter and pointed at me. "Look at her face!"

I didn't want Mary to think I was a spoiled brat too, so I tried to look as though I thought that washing clothes with stale pee was a completely normal thing to do.

Then a truly horrific idea crossed my mind. "But what if it's ... you know ... not just pee in the chamber pots?"

"Then it goes on the dung heap in the garden," said Polly.

The thought of emptying chamber pots on to a dung heap piled with human waste made me feel sick. Turning my head away to avoid smelling or seeing any more than necessary, I lifted the lid of Mrs Bailey's chamber pot and tipped the contents into the already half-full bucket. As Polly and I left the laundry, Mary started to sing again, picking up exactly where she had left off.

"Sings all day, she does," said Polly. "Says it makes the time go quicker."

"Does she work all on her own in there all day? She must be lonely."

"Well, not that lonely," said Polly with a wink. "Not with the stable lads and the gardeners right outside, and no housekeeper watching her like a hawk."

Jacob was grooming a horse outside the stables. Out of the corner of my eye I could see his gaze lingering on me as we crossed the yard. Even after we'd passed him, I could tell his eyes were still fixed on me. It was a relief to get inside and shut the door.

CHAPTER FIFTEEN

In the Housemaid's Closet

Once we had emptied all the chamber pots, scrubbed them out and returned them to the bedrooms, the dressing rooms had to be cleaned again. The dirty water in the washbowls had to be emptied and the bowls scrubbed out and returned to the rooms. Then the bedroom and dressing-room fireplaces had to be cleaned out and relaid, ready for new fires in the evening. My wrists ached, my knees throbbed and my hands were rubbed raw.

"I can't believe we have to do the fires *again*," I said.

"I don't know why they're still wanting fires in this weather," said Polly. "We're waiting every day for the master to give the word. It's a lot easier once the fires stop."

A little clock on the mantelpiece struck the half hour. It was still only half past ten in the morning, and I felt as though I'd done a lifetime's work already.

"Now we need to change our aprons and do the bedrooms," said Polly.

"But we've already done the bedrooms."

Polly roared with laughter. "I'd love to see her face

if we left them in that state."

We traipsed up to our attic room. I was surprised to see a copper can of steaming water on the floor beside the washstand.

"Did you bring this up here?" I asked Polly.

"No, Nell does the servants' rooms."

So poor Nell had to carry hot water cans up four flights of stairs from the basement to the attic.

"Imagine a world," I said, "where nobody has to scrub fireplaces or carry coals and water. Where water comes out of taps by magic, and you just flick a little switch on the wall and the whole house heats up."

Polly reached for the towel. "Wouldn't that be nice? And imagine a world where pigs could fly."

After we had washed our hands and faces, we hung our coal-streaked brown aprons on hooks behind the door and changed into white ones. Then it was back to the bedrooms and dressing rooms, where every surface had to be dusted, every rug brushed on hands and knees, every inch of the floor swept and all the heavy bedclothes put back on the beds perfectly smoothly. By the time we got to the last room, every bone in my body ached and I was ravenous again.

Polly gave me a look of concern as we took our places at either side of the bed. "You look fit to drop."

"No, I'm fine," I said. If I flaked out now, Polly would have to do my work as well as her own. And after all, I was only here for a day. I could put up with it for one day. Poor Polly would have to do this again tomorrow, and the next day, over and over again.

"It's hard at first," Polly said. "I thought I'd die when I started. There were times when I wanted to die. The thought of everlasting sleep sounded like bliss."

"Do you get a lie-in at weekends?" I asked.

"Weekends?" Polly sounded puzzled. Maybe they didn't use that word back then.

"You know, Saturdays and Sundays. Don't you have those days free?"

She looked at me as though I was mad. "Free? Then who'd do all the work? Besides, it's Sunday today, and does this feel like a day off to you?"

"But you must have some days off, surely?"

"Some Sunday mornings we go to church. I always doze off during the sermon, but old Hardwitch pokes me awake with her nasty sharp elbow."

"But don't you get any proper time off? What about holidays?"

Polly's face brightened. "One day last summer we was all allowed the evening off to go to the fair in Lambton. Proper laugh it was. Four men ran a footrace and two of them ran without shirts. One was in breeches and the other had nothing on but a pair of the flimsiest calico drawers you could imagine."

Drawers, I guessed, must mean underwear.

"Well, the ladies said it was disgusting and they turned away and wouldn't watch the race, but me and Eliza, we kept watching – we weren't going to miss the fun for anything. So they all started off, and in the middle of the race the man's drawers burst clean off him. He was crying out as he was running, 'Oh, Lord, oh, Lord, I cannot keep my tackle in, oh, I cannot keep my tackle in!' The ladies were disgusted and they all swept off in their carriages. Eliza and I nearly killed ourselves laughing, and some gentlemen came along and told us we should be ashamed of ourselves. Well, that just made it funnier, of course. We stayed to watch the wrestling afterwards, but that wasn't half so entertaining."

"So," I said, "you're telling me your favourite moment of the whole year was watching a man's underwear fall off at a fair?"

Polly looked thoughtful for a moment. Then she said, "Yes." And we both laughed so hard we nearly fell over.

"Right," she said, giving the quilt a final smoothing down with her hand, "you can sweep the back stairs and I'll do the front. Then we sweep out all the passages and scrub the front steps."

"Do you ever think," I said as we picked up our boxes, "that one day there might be machines to do all this?"

"What do you mean?"

"Well, imagine if there were some contraption that would suck up dirt and dust from floors, without us having to go down on our hands and knees with a dustpan and brush."

"Now, wouldn't that be lovely," she said. "But

since there is no such contraption, you'd better go and sweep the back stairs. Start in the attic and work your way down to the basement."

Sore knees weren't something that had ever bothered me before. Now they were so painful that I couldn't even kneel. I sat on each stair instead, twisting my back to sweep the dust off the stair above me into the dustpan.

As I worked my way down to the ground floor, I heard light footsteps coming up from the hall. I glanced towards them, expecting to see Polly. But it was Alice, walking towards me with a strange glint in her eyes.

"What do you want?" I asked.

She carried on up the stairs as if she hadn't heard. I shunted along the step to let her pass.

As she passed, she kicked out with her left foot and sent the almost-full dustpan clattering downstairs, spilling its contents over every step and sending clouds of dust into the air.

I leapt up with a cry of outrage. "What did you do that for?"

From the top of the stairs, Alice gave a malicious grin. "Oh, dear, what a terrible mess you've made. Now you'll have to sweep it all up again."

"How dare you!" roared Sir Henry's voice from the library.

Alice jumped. Her face turned deathly pale. Then she bolted back down the stairs and sprinted along the corridor towards the kitchen as though a pack of wolves was after her.

Good, I thought. Serves her right. I was sure that shout wasn't aimed at her, but I was glad it shocked her. I was going to have to deal with Alice somehow. I couldn't let her get away with this.

I sat down on the top stair to start clearing up the mess. But I'd barely begun when the sound of raised voices from the library made me stop mid-sweep. This time I could hear Sophia's voice as well as her father's. It sounded as though they were arguing, but I was too far away to make out the words.

Still holding the dustpan and brush, I tiptoed along the corridor until I was right outside the library door.

"Married in two weeks?" said Sophia, her voice shrill and panicky. "But, Father, it is too soon. I pray you, let me wait a while. I am too young."

"Too young?" barked Sir Henry. "You're sixteen. Plenty old enough. Do you think I want you on my hands forever? Your mother was married at fourteen, for goodness' sake."

"Precisely," said Sophia, with a hardness in her voice.

"What the devil do you mean by that?"

"Well, look how much happiness her marriage brought her," she said.

"Happiness! What on earth does happiness have to do with anything?"

Sophia said something in a low voice that I couldn't hear. Sir Henry gave a roar of fury. "Why, you insolent little— Come back here!"

The door was wrenched open. I jumped out of the way as it swung back and crashed against the wall.

Sophia raced out of the room and along the corridor to the back stairs, throwing me a quick scared glance as she passed.

I scuttled to my place on the stairs and started sweeping. I just had time to glimpse Sophia reach the ground-floor hall, open the door of the housemaids' closet and slip inside, before Sir Henry thundered past, almost knocking me down the stairs. At the bottom, he ran along the corridor past the housemaids' closet and flung open the back door. I heard him yelling in the stable yard. Then the door slammed shut again and he stamped back along the corridor and up the stairs. He caught sight of me and glowered.

"You!" he snapped. "Where did she go?" His breath smelled of wine.

"Who, sir?" I asked, trying to look and sound as dim-witted as possible.

His face grew redder and I braced myself for a smack around the head.

"My dratted daughter, imbecile. Where did she go?"

"That way, sir," I said, pointing in the opposite direction from where Sophia went. "I think she was heading upstairs, sir."

He made a sound like a snorting horse and galloped towards the front stairs at the other end of the corridor.

I walked down the back stairs and knocked softly on the door of the housemaids' closet.

There was no sound from inside. I waited for a few seconds and then opened the door.

Pressed against the brooms and buckets, looking ridiculously out of place in her red velvet dress, stood Sophia. Her expression changed from terror to fury as she set eyes on me.

"You?" she spat. "Did I not expressly make it clear that you were never to come near me again?"

It took a real effort to stop myself from telling her that if that was her attitude, she could die in a locked room for all I cared. But then she wouldn't listen to me, and I really had to get my message across and get out of this place. I couldn't stand another day working as a housemaid.

"I told your father you had gone up the front stairs," I said politely. "So you're safe to come out now."

She didn't move. She looked at me through narrowed eyes, as though she was trying to work me out.

"Who are you?" she whispered eventually. "Has my father employed you to spy on me?"

"No!" I said. "I'm just a housemaid. I came from London two days ago. To work here."

She looked at me in silence for a few moments. Then she whispered, "Why did you say what you said to me in the White Parlour this morning? That my father would try to force me to marry Mr Ellerdale?"

"I ... I just heard it. Housemaids hear things, you know."

When she spoke again, she sounded really frightened. "And ... that other thing you said..."

She tailed off, as if she was too scared to finish the sentence.

"About you running away with Robbie?" I said helpfully.

Sophia leapt forward and clamped her hand over my mouth, a look of terror on her face. "Be quiet!" she hissed. She was actually trembling. "Do not ever mention that name again. If my father found out, he would shoot him on the spot."

"Sorry," I said. And I was genuinely sorry, now that I could see how frightened she was. I stepped inside the closet and closed the door, making it pitch black. "I'm sorry," I whispered. "But I'm trying to warn you. You need to run away together. If you refuse to marry Mr Ellerdale, your father—"

Footsteps sounded in the corridor. I held my breath. The footsteps stopped right outside the closet.

"Evie?" It was Polly's voice.

Sophia and I both stood frozen for a second. Then I grabbed all the spare cleaning aprons from their hooks and threw them over Sophia. I heard her stifle a gasp.

"Coming, Polly," I called, and I opened the door a tiny bit, slipped through the gap and closed it firmly behind me.

Polly gave me an exasperated look. "Evie, you drazel, there's dirt all over the stairs and you've left your brush and broom willy-nilly on the steps. If Hardwitch sees that she'll give you a beating you'll never forget, and she'd give me one too, for good measure. I can't be clearing up after you all day. I've got plenty of my own work to be doing. So get on with your jobs, and you'd better work faster than you've ever worked in your life."

I went back to the stairs. Polly bustled off down the corridor. As soon as the kitchen door shut behind her, Sophia slipped out of the cupboard and ran on tiptoes to the back door. She didn't even glance at me. I stood up to run after her and try to speak to her again, but then Mrs Hardwick appeared from the kitchen, looking even more savage than usual, and I had to get back down on my hands and knees.

I seemed to be doomed not to be able to get my message across. In my hour off, I vowed, I would find Robbie in the gardens. Maybe I would have more success with him than I had done with Sophia.

CHAPTER SIXTEEN

A Project
for Polly

As the grandfather clock in the hall struck twelve, Polly appeared, carrying her box and broom. I looked up from the floor I was washing. The cleaning solution had got into the cuts in my hands, and they hurt worse than ever.

Polly smiled at me. "That'll do. Dinnertime."

Dinnertime! I was so hungry I felt faint. The smell of meat had been drifting along the kitchen passage for some time now, making my mouth water.

But as soon as I sat at the table in the servants' hall, a wave of exhaustion came over me. All I wanted to do was lay my head on the table and sleep. My eyelids drooped, my muscles slackened and my mind fogged over.

A thud jolted me upright. Alice had set down a metal plate in front of me, steam rising from the food piled on it: meat in gravy, mashed potato and a huge heap of cabbage. The smell and sight of it woke me up. I was the last to be served and the table was silent except for the sound of eating. Everybody else was clearly as hungry as I was.

Alice came in again with the beer tray. She gave

me a nasty smirk as she pointedly set down a glass of water in front of me. I peered at it suspiciously. I wouldn't have put it past her to have spat in it.

George caught my eye and winked.

"Would milady prefer a glass of Sir Henry's vintage port?" he asked through a mouthful of mashed potato, and roared with laughter at his own joke.

I took an experimental sip of water. It tasted all right and I was really thirsty, so I decided to risk it.

As the eating slowed down, conversations started up, but I was too tired even to listen, let alone talk. The food had made me sleepy again, and I was just closing my eyes when Mrs Hardwick bustled in.

"No dawdling, you two," she said. "There's a pile of mending to be done."

My spirits rose a little. Mending presumably meant sewing, and sewing must mean sitting down.

There was one problem, though. I'd been working since five thirty that morning and I was desperate for a wee. I'd been desperate for some time, but I couldn't face the thought of what it might involve. Now I couldn't wait any longer. But what was the right word?

Then it came back to me – the word Polly had used last night.

"Polly?" I whispered as I followed her down the passage, "where's the privy?"

Polly jerked her thumb over her shoulder. "Little wooden shed behind the stable yard."

In the stable yard, two boys who looked about my age were brushing horses. They said hello to me and

I mumbled hello back. I looked around for Robbie, but I couldn't see him. I would have to find out where he was working so that I could go and speak to him in my hour off.

I walked over to the boys. "Excuse me," I said. "Do you know where Robbie's working this afternoon?"

The boys gaped at me but said nothing. I repeated the question.

"Is she talking foreign?" said one of them to the other. And then to me, "Are you foreign?"

I raised my eyes to heaven. Honestly, how could my accent be so hard to understand?

"Robbie," I said. "Where is he?"

"Ah, Robbie," the boy said. He nodded for several seconds. I waited hopefully. The boy shook his head. "No idea."

"Thanks," I said. "You've been a real help."

I walked through the gap between the stables and the laundry. On a patch of rough ground in the distance stood a ramshackle shed with a heap of soil outside. As I approached, my nostrils caught a foul smell, growing stronger as I drew closer.

I held my breath and opened the door. Inside was a wooden bench balanced on two bales of straw. There was a rough hole in the middle of the bench and, below it, a pit a couple of metres deep. There was no floor, just the muddy ground.

It was a disgusting experience and I got out as quickly as possible. Never again, I thought, will I take flushing toilets for granted.

Jacob was sweeping the yard. He looked up as

I approached, and then ducked into a stable. As I crossed the yard, he reappeared, holding out a battered horseshoe.

"Thought you might like this," he said. "They're lucky, you know."

I looked at him warily, hoping he didn't have a crush on me. Still, it was thoughtful of him. As long as he wasn't expecting anything in return.

"You must hang it this way up, mind," he said, holding the horseshoe in a U shape. "If you hang it upside down, all the luck falls out."

"Thank you," I said, taking the horseshoe.

He nodded and carried on sweeping. The horseshoe was too big for my pocket and I didn't have anywhere to put it, so I knelt down and tucked it behind a flowerpot at the edge of the yard for the time being. As I straightened up, I saw Alice staring at me from the scullery window, a look of absolute loathing in her eyes. But when I walked into the scullery to ask her what on earth her problem was, she had gone.

We did the mending in a little room next to the housekeeper's room on the ground floor. Polly had to sew up rips and tears in lacy petticoats and shirts, while Mrs Hardwick gave me a big cotton sheet to hem. I like sewing, but my sore fingers made it really painful, and it was agony when the thread got caught on my broken skin. The pain was the only thing that kept me awake. That, and thinking about how to deliver my warning to Robbie.

Mrs Hardwick took her work to her own room.

"Has a big fire in there, she does," Polly murmured, "and an endless supply of the family's tea."

There was something in her tone that made me look at her curiously.

"Would you like to be a housekeeper one day?" I asked.

Polly laughed. "Now you're talking about pigs flying again."

"But why not? Why couldn't you be?"

"Well, for one thing, you have to be able to read and write to be a housekeeper."

I stared at her, open-mouthed. I had taken it for granted that Polly could read and write, but I should have remembered from my history lessons that poor children in those days rarely got the chance to go to school.

"So ... they didn't teach you in the workhouse?" I said.

"They didn't waste their time on fancy stuff like that," said Polly. "We had to earn a living." She looked at me. "You was taught your letters, was you?"

"Yes," I said, wondering what the best explanation would be. "My mother taught me."

And as I said that, an idea popped into my head.

"I could teach you," I said. "To read and write."

Polly looked almost frightened. She shook her head. "Oh, no, I could never learn all that."

"Of course you could. If we do a little bit each day, you'll soon learn. And then you could be a housekeeper one day. With your own room and an endless supply of the family's tea."

Polly smiled. "And no more scrubbing out chamber pots or sweeping stairs. I'd be kind to the housemaids too."

"You'd be a lovely boss," I said.

"Boss?" repeated Polly, sounding puzzled.

"Er, sorry, that's another London word. I mean ... employer?"

Polly threw back her head and laughed. "I'd never be an employer, Evie. Mrs Hardwick's not our employer. That's Sir Henry."

I gave up trying to find the right word. "Well, anyway, you'd be a great housekeeper. And I bet she gets paid loads more than you do too."

"Oh, yes," said Polly. "If I was a housekeeper, I'd have a different dress for every day of the week."

"How much do we get paid?" I asked. Not that I was planning to stay long enough to get paid, but I was curious to know.

Polly looked surprised. "Did Hardwitch not tell you? It's eight pounds."

"Eight pounds a week?" I asked, because it obviously wasn't eight pounds an hour, two hundred years ago, or even eight pounds a day, probably.

As soon as I saw Polly's face, I realised I'd made a mistake. I laughed in what I hoped was a convincing way.

"I'm joking!" I said. "I *wish* we got eight pounds a week."

It must be eight pounds a month then, I thought. But I didn't dare ask directly.

"So do you get paid at the end of the month?"

Polly shook her head. "Twice a year. Four pounds on Lady Day and four pounds at Michaelmas."

Eight pounds a *year*?

Polly had to work like this, every single day, for eight pounds a year?

"Hard luck you've just missed Lady Day," she said. "You'll have to wait until September for a new dress now."

CHAPTER SEVENTEEN

Robbie

At three o'clock Mrs Hardwick opened the door from the housekeeper's room.

"One hour off, you two," she said, "and then to the dressing rooms."

"What will you do?" I asked Polly.

"Sleep," she said. "Nell wakes me at four. You coming?"

An hour in bed sounded like bliss. But I had to find Robbie. I needed to pass on my warning today.

"I think I'll go outside for some air," I said.

"I'll show you where you're allowed to walk," said Polly, "and then I'm going to doss down for a bit."

We left by the side door. The air smelled delicious and the gardens were full of birdsong.

"I'll show you the orchard," said Polly. "It's lovely with the blossom out."

Leading off the path behind the house was an arched wooden door, painted pale blue, set into a high brick wall. Polly lifted the latch.

"Oh," I breathed. "It's so beautiful."

We were in a walled garden full of trees, all

covered in clouds of pink and white blossom. Petals floated on the breeze and settled among the drifts of daffodils blooming in the long grass.

I pulled a branch of the nearest tree closer to me, to admire the masses of creamy, pink-tinged flowers. I wished I had my sketchbook, and the time to sit and draw.

"That's apple blossom," said Polly. "And those are pear, and the pink ones are cherries. There's damsons and plums and quinces too. And that's a magnolia over there."

From a high branch a blackbird poured out a stream of song. A robin sat on the wall and looked at me with its perfectly round black eye.

"It's the most beautiful place I've ever seen," I said.

My eye was caught by a big clump of a different plant sprouting from a branch amongst the apple blossom.

"That's mistletoe," said Polly, when I asked her what it was. "We decorate the house with it at Christmas."

Mistletoe! I'd never seen mistletoe actually growing.

There was a movement by the wall. A brown rabbit with a cotton-wool tail was nibbling the grass. Then I saw another one behind it. And a baby! I gazed at them, entranced.

"Rabbits!" I whispered.

Polly laughed. "You're a London girl through and through, aren't you?"

A little auburn creature with a long bushy tail

jumped from a tall tree, landed on the wall and raced along the top of it. Then it stopped, stood on its hind legs and looked at me with its bright black eyes. It was tiny, much smaller than grey squirrels, but its tail was huge.

"Is that a real red squirrel?" I whispered to Polly.

"You never seen a squirrel before?"

"Only grey ones. Never a red one. They're so pretty."

"*Grey* squirrels?" said Polly, and I remembered that grey squirrels only came to England quite recently.

"It's the soot," I said. "London, you know? Everything's grey."

I sat on the grass. There was a dead twig at my feet. I snapped it into pieces and arranged them into the letter P.

"Look, Polly. Do you know what that shape is?"

Polly looked at it and her eyes lit up. "That's a P for Polly. One of the big girls at the silk factory taught me that. Well, I thought she was big, back then. She was nine, I think."

I picked up more twigs, snapped them into pieces and made the rest of her name. "Do you know what that says?"

Polly shook her head.

"That's your name. It says Polly. P-O-L-L-Y."

Polly crouched down and traced the letters with her fingers. "That's my name?"

"Yes." I snapped some more twigs. "There, you do it. Write your name in twigs."

Polly worked fast.

"So now you know those letters," I said. "And then, if you change the first one, you can make another name." I took the twigs she had made into a P and reshaped them. "That's an M. Now it says Molly."

Polly looked intrigued. "So if we put another first letter, we could make Holly."

"Exactly." I shaped the twigs into an H.

"Do you really think you could teach me to read and write?" she said.

"Definitely. You're a quick learner." And then I remembered that I was leaving tonight and not coming back. Nobody was that quick a learner.

Polly yawned. "A little bit each day then. I'm off to bed now. If I don't have a sleep in my hour off, the rest of the day is torture. You coming?"

I shook my head. "I want to explore a bit more. Er, Polly?"

"Yes?"

I was wary of asking the question, knowing how it might sound, but I needed to know the answer.

"Er, Polly, where might the gardeners be working at the moment?"

She looked at me warily. "You stay away from the menservants, Evie. Don't go getting yourself in trouble."

"No, it's not that, honestly. I… I'm trying to avoid them, that's all. I thought maybe we weren't meant to be in the same part of the garden as them."

She didn't look convinced. "I don't know where

they'll be at this time of day. Just make sure you don't go in the formal gardens." She pointed to a door on the far side of the orchard. "That leads to the woods – you're allowed to walk in there, and they're lovely at the moment, with the bluebells out. Just make sure you're back by four."

I walked across the petal-strewn grass, drinking in the flower-scented air, and suddenly I realised why this garden, despite the orchestra of birdsong, had a quality of silence about it that I'd never felt anywhere else.

There was no traffic noise.

In my whole life, I had never been outdoors without hearing traffic. It had never bothered me. I'd never known anything different. But the world was amazing without it. There was a deep sense of peace, as though the earth belonged, not to people and buildings and vehicles, but to the birds and the trees and the growing grass.

I opened the door on the other side of the orchard. And I actually gasped at the sight in front of me.

A shimmering haze of purple covered the ground like a mystical, magical lake. It went on and on and on until it faded into a blue mist on the horizon. From its depths rose the slim, elegant trunks of silver birch trees. A fallen tree trunk, covered with moss, looked as though it was floating on a purple sea. Birds sang all around. A tiny bird, its tail sticking straight up, fluttered out of a bush and landed on the grass in front of me.

I had only seen bluebell woods in pictures. I had never imagined that the real thing would be so amazing.

I wished I could spend the rest of my hour off in this beautiful place, resting my head against the thick springy moss of the fallen tree trunk and inhaling the sweet, earthy scent of the bluebells. But I had to find Robbie.

At the edge of the wood, I stepped through the gap between the stables and the laundry into the sunlight of the stable yard. A breeze drifted towards me and I caught the scent of mint. Instantly I was right back at home, in the kitchen of our flat. Mum always had a pot of mint on the windowsill.

Suddenly home felt very far away.

I looked around and saw a patch of mint growing in a narrow flowerbed outside the scullery. I picked a little sprig and rubbed it between my fingers.

The plant beside the mint smelled lovely as well. And the one next to that was thyme. Mum always grew thyme too.

I plucked a sprig of each herb and put them in my pocket. It would be nice to have something sweet to smell when I was surrounded by less pleasant scents.

As I straightened up, I jumped at the sight of a face at the scullery window. It was Alice again. But this time she wasn't looking at me with hatred. She looked terrified.

I turned around to see what was scaring her. But it was just the peaceful stable yard, nothing frightening at all. There was nobody else around except a boy in a black hat with his back to me, planting seedlings in a border on the other side of the yard.

As I watched, he turned to his left and I saw that it was Robbie. What a piece of luck!

Robbie picked something up from the soil, placed it in his palm and examined it with great attention.

Was it a coin? Or maybe a jewel, dropped by one of the party guests? I walked towards him, curious to find out. He scrambled to his feet.

"Hello," I said. "I'm Evie. The new housemaid."

He smiled at me. He had clear green eyes with little specks of brown in them. "Pleased to meet you, Evie. I'm Robbie, Mr Masters' assistant."

"Mr Masters?"

"The head gardener."

"Oh." I looked at his half-closed palm. "Did you find something?"

He opened his fingers.

"Eugh!" I stepped backwards.

Robbie laughed. "There's no need to be afraid."

"I'm not afraid. It's just … I thought you'd found a jewel or something."

"It is a jewel."

"What?"

"Have a proper look at it and tell me if you don't think it's beautiful."

"You are joking?"

But he seemed perfectly serious. He held out his hand. The slimy wet snail crawled across his palm.

"See the patterns on its shell," he said. "Are they not a thing of beauty? As if they've been painted on with a tiny brush. And look at those delicate markings on its skin. And the antlers, so tiny and so perfect."

"Why do the antlers wave about like that?"

"I think the snail uses them to sense movements in the air – the flutter of a bird's wings, perhaps. Then it can withdraw into its shell and be safe."

I'd always prided myself on being observant, but now, looking at the amazingly intricate designs on the snail's body and shell, I realised that I'd hardly ever looked at anything properly before.

"Lovely, isn't it?" said Robbie. "Snails are perfectly designed. They can protect themselves and keep—"

He stopped and closed his hand over the snail as footsteps approached. Jacob was carrying a bucket of water across the yard. He stopped next to us and set the bucket down. He smelled of body odour and animal dung.

"What you got in your hand, bacon brains?"

"Go away, Jacob," said Robbie.

Jacob pulled Robbie's fingers back and gave a harsh laugh. His breath stank.

"Making a pet of a snail, are you? You're queer in the attic, you are."

With a swift, sudden movement, he grabbed the snail, hurled it to the ground and mashed it into the cobbles with his boot. Then he punched Robbie in the face.

"Stop it!" I screamed.

"Think you're so clever, don't you, louse boy," said Jacob, his face pressed close to Robbie's, "with your book learning and your drawing and your writing? Think you're better than the rest of us. But you're cracked, you are." He tapped the side of his head. "Touched in the upper works. Talking in your sleep again last night, you was. Tossing about on your mattress, crying for your mother. You should be locked up in the asylum, you should."

He shot out his arm and snatched a battered little book from Robbie's jacket pocket.

"Give that back!" shouted Robbie. He made a grab for it, but Jacob held it high above his head.

A huge black dog bounded into the stable yard, barking madly, its tail wagging like a windscreen wiper on full speed. It jumped up at Robbie, knocking Jacob's bucket over. Water splashed over his legs and soaked his leather boots. He let out a furious roar, hurled Robbie's book into the bushes at the edge of the yard, seized a thick stick that was leaning against the stable door and lunged for the dog. Clutching it by the scruff of its neck, he brought the stick down hard on its back. The dog yelped and squirmed, but Jacob had it firmly in his grasp.

"Stop it!" I yelled, but Jacob raised the stick again.

Robbie jumped between Jacob and the cowering, whimpering dog, trying to grab the stick. "Stop it!" he cried. "Give me that!"

But Jacob was taller than Robbie and he held the stick out of reach. "Get out of my way," he said, "or you'll feel it on your back too."

"Go on then, coward," said Robbie. "You just try."

Jacob raised his arm.

"No!" I screamed, jumping for the stick.

Horse's hooves clattered on the cobbles. A long whip swished through the air and cracked across Jacob's backside.

Jacob yelled and leapt up, clutching his buttocks.

Towering above him on a shining black horse, her dark eyes flashing with fury, was Sophia.

She swung down and handed the reins to one of the stable boys, who had hurried across the yard to meet her. In her wine-red velvet dress she looked like a queen in a fairytale. Jacob and Robbie took off their hats and bowed.

Sophia advanced on Jacob, took the stick from his hand and hurled it into a holly bush. She bent down and fondled the whimpering dog, murmuring comforting words in its ear. Then she straightened up to face Jacob, who had his head bowed and his eyes on the ground.

"What is your name?" she demanded.

"Jacob Weston, miss," he mumbled.

"Well, mark my words, Jacob Weston, if I ever see you mistreat a living creature again, you will be dismissed with instant effect. Do you understand me?"

"Yes, Miss Fane," he muttered.

"Now go back to your work. And mind, I shall have you watched."

"Yes, Miss Fane."

He picked up the bucket and walked to the well. As he passed Robbie, he shot him a look of loathing. "You wait," he mouthed. "You just wait."

CHAPTER EIGHTEEN

A Letter

Robbie took no notice of Jacob's threat. He was rummaging in the bushes where Jacob had hurled his book.

Now he emerged, the book in his hand. He walked across the yard towards Sophia.

"Thank you, Miss Fane," he said.

Their eyes met in a gaze so intense that I felt really uncomfortable. I moved back towards the house, wondering what to do now. Luckily Sophia had been so focused on sorting out the Jacob situation, and now she was so focused on Robbie, that she hadn't even noticed me.

Outside the scullery door, I edged between the wall and the clump of bushes. It's not spying, I told myself; it's research. If I was going to help them, I needed to know all I could.

Presumably Sophia wouldn't stay and talk to Robbie for long. She certainly wouldn't want to risk her father or her aunt seeing them together. And once she was gone, I could try to warn Robbie what was about to happen, and hopefully he could persuade her to run away with him. Before it was too late.

I noticed a folded sheet of paper lying on the ground under the bushes. I picked it up and unfolded it.

It was covered in the most beautiful pen-and-ink drawings. A feather, so detailed that I wanted to reach out and stroke it. A snail, every marking on its shell perfectly captured in pen and ink. A branch of apple blossom. A bird's nest, woven in grass and moss, with four speckled eggs inside it.

I turned the paper over. The other side was quite different. It showed two young children, a boy and a girl, stick-thin and dressed in rags, hunched over some sort of machine. Behind them stood a huge, glowering man, brandishing a stick. Above them hovered an angelic figure. In the speech bubble coming from its mouth were the words:

A robin redbreast in a cage
Puts all Heaven in a rage.

Had Robbie drawn these? I glanced over at him. He and Sophia still stood facing each other, motionless, their eyes locked together.

Now Sophia shifted her gaze from Robbie's eyes to the book in his hand.

"Your Shakespeare," she said. "Oh, I hope it is not damaged."

"No," said Robbie. "All is well."

He flicked through the pages. "I have something for you," he murmured. "Some sketches."

His forehead creased into a frown as he flicked through the book again. "They were here. I tucked them in the book. They must have fallen out."

I dropped the sheet of paper to the ground. I edged it out from beneath the bush with my toe and then quickly withdrew my foot. Robbie looked around the yard and saw it.

"Oh, there it is," he said. I drew myself further back into the bush as he retrieved the paper and handed it to Sophia.

She studied the drawings in silence for a while. Then she gazed at Robbie in awe. "These are exquisite," she said.

She turned the sheet over and read the lines of poetry above the picture of the starving children.

"William Blake," she murmured. "My father burned my copy of Blake's poems. He says Mr Blake is an insane revolutionary. But it does not signify. I have the poems here." And she tapped the side of her head.

She hesitated, as if trying to pluck up the courage to say something. Then she glanced around the yard. I shrank back against the wall. Sophia must have been satisfied that nobody was watching, because she took a folded piece of paper from her pocket and handed it to Robbie.

"Read it as soon as you can," she said in a low voice.

He stuffed it in his jacket pocket, just as the back door opened and Nell walked out with a bucket of vegetable peelings. Sophia turned and swept away across the cobbles towards the front of the house. The stable clock struck four. I emerged from my hiding place, brushed the cobwebs from my clothes and slipped inside.

My heart beat fast as I went to collect my box from the housemaids' closet. What was on that piece of paper? Sophia had told Robbie to read it as soon as he could. So it must have been important. Was it a letter about their running away together? Had Sophia actually taken notice of what I'd said?

Deep in thought, I almost bumped into Alice in the passage. Terror flooded her face. She pressed herself into the wall and clenched her fists.

"Are you all right?" I asked.

"Quite well, I thank you," she murmured. She kept her face lowered and didn't look at me.

I shrugged and walked on.

"Good day to you," said Alice, still pressed against the wall.

"Good day," I said, thinking I had never met anyone so weird in my whole life.

Polly appeared from the other direction. "Dressing rooms again," she said, opening the housemaids' closet and handing me my box. "Fires lit, slops emptied, chamber pots scoured, everything dusted and cleaned, and hot and cold water for the washstands. Then, while they're dressing for dinner, we tidy all the downstairs rooms and stoke up the downstairs fires. We bolt down a bit of supper while they're having their dinner, before we go up and get the bedrooms ready."

Listening to the endless list of jobs made me even more determined to find out what was in that letter. If Sophia and Robbie really were planning to run away today or tomorrow, then my job was done, and I wouldn't have to come back here for another day of drudgery. Perfect.

But I couldn't ask either of them directly what was in the letter, because obviously neither of them was going to tell a random housemaid about their forbidden secret love affair. So how could I find out?

I racked my brains as I worked, earning several scoldings from Polly for my half-hearted efforts. By suppertime, I thought I was actually going to die from exhaustion.

"No fires tomorrow," said Mrs Hardwick, as Alice appeared with the beer tray.

"Thank the Lord for that," said Polly. "That'll make our lives easier, Evie."

Mrs Hardwick gave a disapproving grunt. "Don't you two think you're going to have an easy time of it. The chimney sweep is coming tomorrow, so all the rooms will need to be dust-sheeted and all the carpets taken up first thing in the morning. You can give the carpets a good beating out of doors while the sweep's at work."

Polly winked at me. "Heaven forbid we should look forward to an easier life," she murmured.

Alice shrieked. The mugs rattled on the tray and beer slopped over the edges.

"Alice, really!" snapped Mrs Hardwick. "Whatever is the matter?"

Alice's face was white. William jumped up, took the tray from her and sat her down on the bench.

"What is it?" he asked. "What happened?"

Alice shot a terrified glance at me, but when our eyes met, she instantly looked away. Shakily, she pointed at a glowing coal on the hearth. "It spat out of the fire," she whispered, "right in front of me. And look at the shape. Like a... Like a coffin!" she finished in a frightened little squeak.

George laughed. "You don't want to be taking any heed of that nonsense," he said.

But Mary and Betty were looking uneasily at me.

"What?" I asked. "What have I done?"

"Nothing," said Polly. "Take no notice."

But I was sure there was something Polly wasn't telling me. I was glad when supper was over, even though that only meant more work. The atmosphere in the servants' hall was so weird, and I had no idea why. It was almost like they were frightened of me. But why on earth would they be frightened of an incompetent housemaid?

After supper, the dressing rooms had to be cleaned again, the fires stoked up, the chamber pots emptied and the washing water changed for the third time that day. Then we had to get the bedrooms ready for the night.

"Honestly," I said, as Polly showed me how to turn down the bedclothes so they were perfectly placed for Mrs Bailey to get into bed, "can't these people do anything for themselves? I'm surprised we don't have to undress them."

Polly looked shocked. "They wouldn't let us get that close. It's their lady's maids and valets what undresses them."

I gaped at her. "They actually do have someone to undress them? I was joking!"

Polly looked at me, her face scrunched up in puzzlement. "You must have had someone to undress you though, when you lived in London."

"Oh, er, yes, of course," I said. "But ... not quite the same," I added lamely.

Polly was still giving me a funny look, so I asked, "Where are these ladies' maids and valets then? How come I haven't seen them? Where do they have their meals?"

"Oh, they don't come near the servants' hall. They're far too grand for us. If Mrs Bailey's maid passes me in the passageway, she wrinkles her nose like I've offended her nostrils. Wouldn't even look at me, let alone pass a civil word."

I remembered the woman who had come out of Sophia's dressing room the first time I came into the past. She must have been Sophia's lady's maid. The one she'd mentioned, with the French name.

By ten o'clock, when we finally lit our candles and trudged up to the attic, I felt like a sleepwalker. I could barely reach up to take the pins out of my hair, and I didn't even try to wrestle with the buttons on my dress. I just tugged my boots off and flopped into bed.

A whole day of drudgery, and for what? I had completely failed to get my message across to Sophia or Robbie. Unless – and I really, really hoped this was the case – unless Sophia actually *had* listened to my warning, and the letter that she had given to Robbie had been about plans to run away together.

I would just have to come back tomorrow night and find out. And maybe they would already have run away by then. So I would just have to survive one more day of drudgery before I could go back to the twenty-first century forever. Well, one more day wouldn't kill me. After all, poor Polly had to do this every single day of her life.

Anna had promised to take me to the records office in Highfield tomorrow. I would look up Sophia and Robbie, and try to find out more about them. I wasn't sure how that would help, but I might find something useful. And I could take my phone to be repaired too, if it still wasn't working.

And when I came back here tomorrow night, if Sophia and Robbie were still here, somehow I would have to convince them to escape.

Before it was too late.

CHAPTER NINETEEN

The Climbing Boys

Somebody was shaking my shoulders.

"Evie! Evie! Lord, you're a sound sleeper. Come on, lazybones, it's after five."

My cocoon was ripped apart as the blankets were pulled back and cold air hit me. I squealed and grabbed at the bedclothes, but I couldn't reach them. With a growl of frustration, I sat up and opened my eyes.

Polly, fully dressed, was standing over me, laughing.

"Stir along, sleepyhead, there's work to be done. Just as well you went to bed in your clothes; that'll save a few minutes. Get your apron on and splash your face with some of that water. You're lucky you didn't get the basin emptied on your head. I did think about it, but I decided to go easy on you, seeing as you're new and all."

I stared down at my clothes, my heart beating wildly under my corset.

I had gone to bed in these clothes.

And now I'd woken up in them.

But... But ...

"Polly?"

"Mm?"

"What day is it?"

Polly laughed. "I've never met such a simpleton. It was Sunday yesterday, so today must be Monday, unless the world's gone very far awry."

"Monday the twenty-sixth of April?"

"Lord love you, yes. Sweep's coming this morning, so look sharp and put your boots on. We need to get the place dust-sheeted."

I couldn't move. My head was pounding so hard I thought I'd faint if I tried to get up.

Why was I still in the past? Why was I not in Anna's flat?

"Evie, if you don't get out of bed this minute, that bowl of water is going right over your head."

She reached for the bowl. I swung my feet out of bed and forced them into my boots, wincing as the leather rubbed my blisters. I tied the laces, my head spinning.

Why was I here? Why had the magic not worked?

Polly flung the brown apron into my lap. "Evie, stir yourself. Do you really want to lose your job?"

I sprang to my feet. I couldn't lose my job. If I had to leave Charlbury, then how would I ever get back to the present?

For the next three hours I went through the motions of work (getting clouted twice in the process for not doing things thoroughly enough – thank you, Mrs Hardwick), while desperately trying to work out why I was still in the past and how I could get back to my own time.

The only explanation I could come up with was that I had made a promise. I had promised the ghost of Sophia that I would help her. So maybe – and this did sound crazy, even in my head – maybe the ghost wouldn't let me go back to my time until I had changed things in Sophia's time. Maybe Sophia had to escape from Charlbury before I could escape from the past.

But then my blood ran cold with a horrible thought. What if Sophia *didn't* manage to escape? She was going to be locked up tomorrow. So if my theory was right, Sophia would have to escape from Charlbury today if I were to have any chance of going back to the twenty-first century.

So I had to make absolutely sure that she did. Otherwise…

No. I couldn't even let myself think about that.

When Polly and I walked into the servants' hall for breakfast, Alice, Mary and Betty were standing in a huddle at the far end of the room. Alice was clearly telling the others some shocking piece of news.

"And when I looked again," she said in a hushed voice, "the tallow was rising right up the wick of my candle."

Mary frowned. "What does that signify?"

"It's a winding sheet," said Betty. "Foretells a death in the family, they say."

"I tell you," said Alice in an urgent whisper, "she's—"

Betty caught my eye, flushed and nudged Alice. "Shh."

All three of them glanced at me, then looked away. The huddle broke up and Mary and Betty sat down for breakfast, keeping their eyes on the table.

"Good morning, Evie," said Alice in that same carefully polite way she had spoken to me yesterday.

"Good morning," I replied.

Alice edged out of the room with her fists clenched, keeping close to the wall.

"What's going on?" I asked the others.

They glanced at each other awkwardly and looked back at their plates. I looked at Polly, but she was studying her plate too.

This was horrible. I didn't mind so much about the others, but I couldn't bear it if Polly turned against me.

The door from the beer cellar opened and Mrs Hardwick came in, followed by William and George. She frowned at the table as the men sat down.

"No bread? Where's that slattern of a kitchen maid?"

"Here, Mrs Hardwick," panted Alice, rushing in with the bread board and butter dish. She set them in the middle of the table. Then she froze, her face white.

"What is it, girl?" asked Mrs Hardwick.

"Do you not hear?"

Everyone listened. Outside, a dog howled.

"Must be the chimney sweep's dog," said George. "Poor thing, looks half starved. He's tied it up behind the stables."

"What on earth's got into you?" Mrs Hardwick asked the white-faced Alice. "Pull yourself together, girl, and get back to your work."

As Alice passed Mary and Betty on her way out, she whispered, "Did you hear that? Another portent." She glanced fearfully at me as she scuttled from the room.

I looked at Betty and Mary.

"What's a portent?"

They kept their eyes on the table, but William muttered, "Some do believe that a howling dog signifies a death in the family."

Mary crossed herself. George snorted. "Stuff and nonsense. You surely don't believe that?"

"Quite right," said Mrs Hardwick. "I don't want to hear any more of this silly gossip. Where on earth has it come from?"

After breakfast, Polly and I had to clean up after the sweeps. We folded the heavy dustsheets and carried them outside to shake off the soot. Then we put the carpets back in place and dusted all the surfaces.

I hadn't seen so much as a glimpse of Sophia all morning. I had to find an opportunity to speak to her and warn her properly.

Or maybe I could write her a note? My heart gave a little leap of hope. That might work. Even if she tore it up in a rage, surely she would at least read it first?

I just had to find a sheet of paper and a pen, and

that shouldn't be too hard.

Terrifying thoughts kept sneaking into my head.

What if I was trapped here forever? What if it didn't even have anything to do with Sophia? What if I had fallen through some crazy hole in time and this was now my life?

Mrs Hardwick appeared as I was dusting the ornaments on Mrs Bailey's dressing table and taking the opportunity to look out of the window. On the path outside, talking to Mr Paxton, the butler, stood a huge, soot-blackened man who must be the chimney sweep.

"As soon as you've finished in here," Mrs Hardwick said, "go and wash the floors in the basement passages and scrub all the steps."

After she had left the room, I took the opportunity to check Mrs Bailey's drawers and cupboards for paper and pens. But half of them were locked and the rest had nothing in them of any use to me. I would have to keep looking.

I trudged downstairs, dreading the thought of spending hours on my knees on a cold stone floor with the cleaning solution stinging the cuts on my hands.

As I walked through the ground-floor hall, I heard a scrabbling noise. I stopped and listened. It seemed to be coming from the Oak Parlour.

More scrabbling, and then a bump and a clattering of metal. Then a little cry.

I ran into the parlour. In the fireplace, scrambling to his feet amid a clutter of fallen fire irons, was a very small boy. From the top of his head to the tips of his toes, he was completely black with soot. Dark-red patches of blood oozed from cuts and sores all over his body. He wore nothing but threadbare shorts and a shirt, both ripped to rags and as black as his skinny body. Even the whites of his big, frightened-looking eyes weren't white, but red. They looked so sore that it hurt me to see them.

The boy gave a hacking cough. "Has my master gone?" he asked in a croaky, breathless voice, and coughed again. "Has he left?"

I realised that my horror at his terrible state must show in my face. I tried to speak cheerfully.

"I think he's just outside. Shall I take you to him?"

He looked at me blankly. Maybe he couldn't make out my accent. His own was very strong, but I was getting used to the local accent by now. I repeated my words, speaking slowly and clearly, and imitating Polly's voice as well as I could. This time he seemed to understand. He looked more frightened than ever as he nodded.

"Yes, please, miss. He'll get in a terrible rage if I'm late. I got stuck, you see. That chimney there –" he pointed to the fireplace behind him "– is as crooked as a corkscrew up inside, and I got wedged in a little twisted passage, so that I couldn't hardly get myself out of it. I thought I was going to be stuck there forever, miss."

It must have been an incredibly narrow passage if this poor little boy had got stuck in it. I'd never seen anyone so skinny in my life.

I took his soot-blackened hand and led him out of the room. As we came into the passage, Sophia appeared from the Hall, looking stunning in a pale-blue dress. When she saw the boy, she froze.

"Who is this?"

"He's the chimney sweep's boy, Miss Fane."

I thought she might order me away, but she didn't even look at me. Horror at the state of the boy seemed to be the only thing on her mind.

"How old are you?" she asked him.

"Five, madam," he said, and gave that hacking cough again.

"You look starved," said Sophia. "Are you hungry?"

He nodded.

Footsteps sounded in the corridor and another boy limped into the passage. He was slightly taller, and just as ragged and black. He carried a stiff-bristled brush with short handles and some sort of scraping tool.

Fear spread over his face as he saw Sophia. "Oh, I'm sorry, madam, but my master is waiting and he's in a fair rage. I must take my brother back to him. We have another house to do, and it's a fair few miles to walk."

Sophia crouched in front of the older boy.

"What is your name?" she asked gently.

"John, madam."

"Tell me, John, does your master give you enough to eat?"

The boy looked afraid. He glanced over his

shoulder. "No, madam," he whispered. "Just a bit of dry bread in the morning and again at night."

"And does he beat you?"

Again, he looked around before whispering, "Yes, madam, all the time."

"Why do you stay with him?"

"We are apprenticed to him, madam, me and my brother. We ran away, back to my father's house, but my father was afraid to let us stop, as he might be summoned, as we are bound as apprentices for seven years."

"And where do you sleep?"

"On a heap of sacks in the cellar, ma'am."

Sophia looked at his threadbare clothes. "But you must be so cold in winter."

"Yes, madam. But the worst thing is that my master won't allow us to wash, not ever, so we are very sore with the clogged stuff that has almost eat into our flesh, see."

He lifted his ragged shirt to reveal oozing sores. Sophia and I both winced.

At this moment, Polly came clattering down the stairs, her box in one hand and a broom in the other. Sophia turned to her.

"Polly, take these boys to the kitchen and fetch Mrs Hardwick. Ask her to look after them."

"Oh, begging your pardon, madam," said the older boy, "but we cannot stay. Our master will be angry."

"Do not concern yourselves with your master," said Sophia. "I will deal with your master. You go and eat."

"Come with me," said Polly, smiling her kind smile and holding out a hand to each of the boys.

Sophia straightened up. Her cheeks were flushed and her face was set and determined. I followed her down the stairs to the basement, making the most of the fact that I seemed to be invisible to her this morning. I wanted to see how she was going to deal with the chimney sweep.

I lurked in the doorway as Sophia strode into the stable yard, where the huge, grim-faced man I had seen from the window was talking to Mr Paxton, the butler. The sweep was as soot-coated as the boys, but better dressed, in a rough jacket and breeches with boots.

Beyond them, Robbie was planting in a flower bed. At the sound of Sophia's shoes on the cobbles, he looked round. His cheeks reddened and he turned back to his work.

Could I sneak over and speak to Robbie? But the others were standing right in the middle of the stable yard, exactly between us, and one of them would be bound to see me and order me back in before I had a chance to say anything.

Sophia marched over to the sweep.

"Are you responsible for those two wretched boys in there?"

His expression darkened. "Are they making a nuisance, madam? Where are they? I sent the older one in to fetch his brother, and now they've both disappeared. I'll show them what happens to idle wretches like them."

Sophia's dark eyes flashed.

"You will not lay a finger on either of them," she said, her voice trembling with anger. "You will never see them again."

He stared at her. "Those boys are apprenticed to me."

"They are not apprentices," said Sophia. "They are your slaves."

"They're my lawful property for seven years."

"You shall be fully compensated for your loss," said Sophia. "I shall buy their freedom."

Robbie was crouched motionless over the flower bed, holding a seedling in mid-air, its soil-coated roots dangling.

"And what about the other chimneys that has to be done this morning," the sweep growled, "and one so twisted that none but shrimps such as they can crawl up it?"

"I shall send a footman to the house," said Sophia, "and explain that you will be back tomorrow with a set of brushes, which you will find quite as quick and convenient as your climbing boys. More so, I dare say, since brushes cost nothing to keep. Not that I imagine it costs you a great deal to keep those poor children."

"And where am I supposed to find money for brushes?"

"I shall have the brushes ordered today and sent to you."

He shook his head. "I shall lose all my trade,

madam, if I have only brushes. Folks want boys. Boys is better, see, for getting into awkward places."

"I shall see that you do not lose your trade," said Sophia grandly. "And mind, Mr Paxton knows where you live, and if you ever send a child up a chimney again, I shall ensure that not a house in the neighbourhood uses your services. Is that quite clear?"

He looked stupefied. "Yes, madam."

"Good. Now leave."

He gave a quick nod. "Yes, madam."

Robbie glanced up from his work as Sophia walked back into the house. I could dash across the cobbles and give him my warning now, I thought. But before I had taken two steps, the head gardener appeared around the corner and called him. Robbie straightened up and they walked off together towards the formal gardens.

Blast.

I walked back indoors and lurked just outside the kitchen door. Mrs Winter, sour-faced as usual, started at the sight of Sophia in her embroidered silk dress, sweeping across the kitchen flagstones. She bowed her head and gave an awkward curtsey, almost toppling over in the attempt.

"Good morning, Miss Fane," said Mrs Winter.

"Mrs Winter, would you make up a large parcel of food for the climbing boys to take home?" said Sophia. "Bread, cheese, eggs, cold meats, and so on."

"Very good, Miss Fane," said Mrs Winter, bobbing another wobbly curtsey.

"Where is Mrs Hardwick?" asked Sophia.

"She went to inspect the dairy, madam."

Sophia marched out of the kitchen and along the corridors. I followed her, unwilling to miss anything. Luckily, nobody seemed to notice me when Sophia was around. They only had eyes for her.

Mrs Hardwick came out of the dairy. "Well, how lovely to see you down here, Miss Fane," she said with a warm smile. It was the first time I'd seen her smile. She looked completely different.

To my astonishment, Sophia gave her a big hug. It must have been like hugging a lamp-post.

"I only wish I were able to spend more time here," Sophia said, "but you know how it is."

"Indeed I do, madam. But you are looking very well, I must say."

"How are the little boys?" asked Sophia.

"Come and see for yourself, madam. I've sat them in the servants' hall."

"Thank you. And, Mrs Hardwick, pray do not mention this to my father. There is no need for him to know about it."

The boys sat hunched at the long table, gnawing their way through huge hunks of bread and cheese. They scrabbled to their feet as Sophia walked towards them. Mrs Hardwick poured milk into two mugs and set them on the table. Then she noticed me for the first time.

"What do you think you're doing, hanging around like a simpleton?" she snapped. "Get back to your work."

I left the room. In the doorway, I glanced back. Sophia was smiling at the boys.

"Sit down and enjoy your meal," she said. "I just need you to tell me where you live."

The hunted, frightened looks came over their faces again.

"Not the sweep's house," she reassured them. "Your father's house. Once you have eaten, Mrs Hardwick will see to it that you are given baths and that your sores are treated with ointment." She looked at Mrs Hardwick, who nodded. "And after that," said Sophia, "we are going to take you home."

CHAPTER TWENTY
The Spider's Web

That afternoon, Polly and I spent our sewing time making clothes for the climbing boys to wear home. While we worked, I formed letters from scraps of thread for Polly to learn, starting at the beginning of the alphabet. It was better than nothing, but it was a bit fiddly.

"We need a pen and paper really," I said. "Where could we get some?"

"Pen and paper!" said Polly. "You'd be lucky! You surely didn't learn to write with pen and paper?"

"No, of course not," I said, wondering what I should have learned to write with.

"There'll be chalk in the farmyard," said Polly. "The Downs is all made of chalk. There's always bits lying about."

Chalk. Of course.

"That would be perfect," I said, thinking it would be perfect for teaching Polly, but not quite so useful for writing a secret note to Sophia.

"We'll get some tomorrow," said Polly. "I need a sleep now. Coming?"

"I'm going to have a walk first," I said. "I'll

see you later."

This time I didn't ask her if she wanted to come with me. This hour off might be the last chance I had to make sure Robbie and Sophia got away from Charlbury today. And my best hope of getting my message across was surely to speak to Robbie. He just thought I was a housemaid who had tried to help him stop Jacob from beating the dog yesterday. He might not take any notice if I warned him, but it was worth a try. I might at least get to finish my message before he sent me away.

I walked all around the house but I couldn't see Robbie anywhere. Eventually, just beyond the orchard, I came to another arched door in the wall. Maybe this was the kitchen garden that Polly had mentioned.

I lifted the latch and opened the door.

Inside the garden, grassy paths crisscrossed dozens of neatly dug beds, where rows of little green shoots poked through the crumbly soil. Fruit trees blossomed against old brick walls and the occasional petal, like stray confetti, twirled in the breeze. Along the far wall ran a long, low greenhouse.

At first I thought there was nobody there. But then I spotted him, half hidden by bushes, kneeling on the path at the far end of the garden. There was nobody else around.

I couldn't believe it. I actually had a proper opportunity to give Robbie my warning. And I had plenty of time too. I wouldn't need to terrify him by blurting it out. I could spend some time talking to him to gain his trust first and then gradually get to the real message.

Finally it looked as though luck was on my side.

I walked across to Robbie, trying to look casual and friendly, not like somebody about to deliver a warning from the future.

Beside him lay an open sketchbook, a quill pen and a bottle of ink. But he wasn't drawing. He was staring intently at a leafless bush.

He looked up as I approached, and smiled as he recognised me.

"Come and look at this," he said softly. "Is it not the most beautiful thing you ever saw?"

Having been lured into worshipping a snail yesterday, I was prepared for "the most beautiful thing you ever saw" to be anything from a molehill to a rabbit dropping. So I was quite relieved when I followed his pointing finger to see an enormous spider's web. And there was something about Robbie that made me want to see the world through his eyes. So I crouched next to him and looked.

The perfectly woven web was suspended, as if by magic, between the twigs. Hundreds of dewdrops, fat little spheres, perched on the almost invisible threads, like pearls on lace. As the web blew softly backwards and forwards in the breeze, the threads stretched, but the dewdrops miraculously stayed in place. On the surface of each dewdrop sat a tiny rainbow.

"Perfect, isn't it?" murmured Robbie.

"It's amazing."

"Those threads look so delicate, don't they? But see how strong they are. The wind blows them but they never snap."

We watched in silence for a minute, as the web bent in the breeze, the dewdrops glittering as they caught the sunlight. It really was beautiful.

"I was going to draw it," said Robbie, "but I got caught up just looking at it. And now I must get back to work."

I glanced at the open page of his sketchbook. The drawing was unfinished but I immediately recognised the tiny chimney sweep. Robbie had captured perfectly his skinny, battered body and frightened face. Above it, he had written:

How the chimney sweeper's cry
Every blackening church appals

William Blake

Robbie stood, rolled up his sleeves and took his spade from where it was stuck in the ground. He moved over to an empty bed and started digging, turning the soil over in great clods. I walked over and stood a few metres away from him, watching.

His arms were covered in scars, and I wondered how he had got them. It would be insensitive to ask, I decided. But then I remembered that he would be leaving Charlbury today, and this was the last opportunity I would ever have to talk to him.

"Those scars on your arms," I said. "What happened?"

Robbie carried on digging as though he hadn't heard me, although he must have done.

"Sorry," I said. "I shouldn't have asked."

I stayed where I was as he continued to dig.

"I was apprenticed to a farmer," he said eventually, without looking up.

"Apprenticed? Like the climbing boys?"

"I was a little older. I was bound to him when I was eight, for seven years. I had my board and lodging, but no wages."

"No wages? In seven years?"

"Apprentices are often little more than slaves. It is the same for those poor climbing boys – or it was, until Miss Fane bought their freedom." His cheeks reddened and he stopped.

"Did they give you enough to eat?" I asked, picturing the poor half-starved chimney sweeps.

He shook his head as he drove the spade into the ground again. "I had a bit of dry bread at breakfast and another at dinner. I was hungry all the time."

"What sort of work did you do?"

"Everything that needed doing. Milking was the best job, even though I had to get up at half past two in summer to get the cows in. I could sit on a stool to do the milking, and sometimes I would drink a bit of milk, if no one was about, straight out of the bucket. Beautiful it was, warm and creamy. Then I had to feed the pigs and muck them out. After breakfast, I went into the fields. I had to drive the plough, pick stones, weed, sow corn and reap it, dig potatoes, hoe turnips. Pulling turnips, when snow was lying about, that was the worst job. My fingers were like ice and I was frozen half to death. Terrible bleeding chilblains I had, all winter long, so sore and itchy they made you want to cry, but you mustn't scratch them, for scratching makes them worse."

"That sounds awful," I said. However sore my hands were, at least I didn't have to pull turnips in the snow. "And where did you sleep? Did you stay in their house?"

"Oh, no, I never went in the house. I slept on a heap of sacks in the stable loft." He dug in silence for a while, and then he said, "The loneliness was the worst thing. To have nobody to talk to, from dawn until dusk, not to have one kind word, year after year: that is very hard for a child."

"And the farmer beat you?" I asked, thinking of the scars.

He nodded. "My master and my mistress had very bad tempers. Several times a week, my mistress would throw me on the ground, hold me by the ears, kneel upon me and beat me until I screamed."

"Do you not have any parents?" I asked. Surely no parents would have allowed their son to be treated like that for seven years.

"My father died when I was young. And my mother and sisters had to work too. My sisters worked in the silk factory in the village, and my mother spun wool at home."

I noticed he was using the past tense. "Are they… Do they still live in the village?"

He took a deep breath. "My sisters caught a fever at the factory. And then my mother caught it too…" He stopped digging and gazed into the distance. His eyes were wet. "A neighbour brought the news to my master's house. I was not allowed to attend the funeral. My master said there was no need and I had better spend the time being useful."

He drew his sleeve across his face and started digging again.

"But I was very fortunate," he said. "After the funeral, my aunt came to the farm to visit me, and she was so shocked that she bought my freedom. It was she who found me my first job as gardener's boy, at Lord Northbridge's place."

"And what was that like?" I asked.

Robbie's eyes lit up. "It was like Heaven. The people were so kind. Lord Northbridge's steward, Mr Allen, was a very good man. When he saw that I liked to learn, he lent me a primer, so that I could teach myself to read. And then he gave me the free use of his library." He smiled. "That library was a magic kingdom to me. I taught myself to draw using the books in there and studying the prints. I felt as though whole new worlds were opening up to me. It gave me such a thirst for knowledge. I feel constantly in a hurry. There is just not enough time to read and learn all that I wish to learn." He hesitated. "But it is more than that. I… I want to do something – to change things."

"What sort of things?"

"Those climbing boys... There are so many other children who suffer a similar plight, in factories and mines and on the land. We—" He stopped and blushed again. "I want to campaign for their slavery to end. Imagine a world where all children were able to go to school. Imagine the difference that could be made to children's lives if they were able to read and write, instead of slaving in factories and mines."

"That time will come, I'm sure," I said. It felt really good to be sure of something for once. "When all children go to school until they're sixteen."

"Sixteen!"

"It will be the law."

"But how would their parents afford it?"

"The government will pay. Out of taxes."

Robbie smiled as he turned over a great clod of soil. "Imagine a time when the government spends tax money on education instead of war. It sounds like paradise."

The idea of school being paradise was a new one to me, but, compared with childhood in 1814, I suppose it was.

The garden door opened and Mr Masters appeared, wheeling a barrow. Suddenly I was filled with panic. If I didn't get my message across now, then Sophia would be locked up tomorrow. And if Sophia was locked up, then I would have failed to keep my promise to her ghost. And then ... would I be stuck in the past forever?

"What is wrong, Evie?" asked Robbie, looking at

me with concern. "You look frightened."

I moved closer to him. "I... I came to warn you," I whispered. "Please, Robbie, you must believe me. You and Soph— Miss Fane – you must run away together, tonight."

At the mention of Sophia's name, Robbie turned completely white. He stared at me, his eyes huge with terror.

"I'm sorry to frighten you," I hurried on, "but I've heard things, and I know Miss Fane is going to refuse to marry Mr Ellerdale and then her father will lock her in her room for the rest of her life. It's going to happen very soon. So if you want to be together, you must get away tonight, before he locks her up."

Robbie still looked petrified, but now there was a look of determination on his face too.

"Go," he said. "Say nothing of this to anybody, I beg you."

"Robbie, please trust me," I begged. "Please. I know what will happen if—"

"You!" shouted Mr Masters. I whipped round to see him glaring at me from the other side of the garden. "Get out of my garden and back to your work."

His garden? Ha! Sir Henry would have loved it if he had heard that. I was about to answer back but I bit my tongue just in time. I didn't want him to chase me out of the garden. I needed more time with Robbie. So I curtsied politely and said, "I came to deliver a message from Mrs Hardwick, actually. I'm just about to leave."

Without waiting for his reaction, I turned back to Robbie. "Please, Robbie," I whispered. "I swear this is true. I've heard it from people who know. How can I—"

He held out his hand to stop me.

"We... I... We have plans," he whispered. "Thank you, Evie. You must go."

Mr Masters came striding across the path towards me, his face scarlet with fury.

"Calm down, I'm going," I said to him.

I turned back to Robbie. "Today," I whispered. "It's urgent. You must go today. Believe me, please."

Mr Masters was advancing on me. I hitched up my skirts and raced down the path and out of the garden before he could hit me. He looked like he had a pretty strong right arm.

Once I was at a safe distance, I slowed down and walked back to the house. My stomach was churning. What had Robbie meant by, "We have plans"? Was that what Sophia's letter had been about? What were these plans? Did they realise how urgent it was that they got away tonight?

As I crossed the stable yard, my head was so full of our conversation that when I became dimly aware of shouting and stamping and jingling sounds, they seemed to be coming from another world. But then the sounds grew louder and louder, closer and closer, until they became a frantic clattering and creaking and crunching of gravel.

Around the corner galloped two glossy white horses, pulling a gleaming black carriage. On a high seat at the front of the carriage sat Charles Ellerdale.

"Whoa! Steady on, steady on!" he shouted, yanking at the reins.

But the horses didn't steady on. And, in a chaotic blur of neighing and kicking and gravel and wheels, I realised they were hurtling straight towards me.

Just in time, I dived out of their path, crashing headlong on the grass beside the drive. The carriage careered to a stop, horses whinnying, harness clanking.

Charles Ellerdale leapt from the driver's seat, almost landing on me, and handed the reins to Jacob, who had hurried out of the stable block.

I looked up at that vast stomach with the straining waistcoat buttons. He glanced down at me contemptuously.

"Get out of my way," he barked, swinging his leg back. I gasped as I felt a sharp pain in my side. He strutted off towards the front door, leaving me staring, open-mouthed and speechless, at his retreating back.

I struggled to my feet, my heart pounding.

"Did you see that?" I said to Jacob.

"See what?"

"He kicked me! I was lying on the ground and he actually kicked me!"

Jacob shrugged. "You were in his way."

I gaped at him for a moment. Then I said, "Serves me right, I guess, expecting sympathy from someone who beats dogs for fun."

I turned to leave, but he grabbed my wrist.

"Get off me," I said, trying to shake off his hand. But he grasped my wrist tighter and pulled me towards him. I could smell his rotten breath.

"Don't think I haven't noticed," he murmured.

My heart started beating very fast. I tried to keep my voice casual. "Noticed what?"

"You know what."

"I have no idea what you're talking about."

"Sneaking off to the kitchen garden to see that bacon-brained simpleton."

"He's not a simpleton!"

Fury flashed across Jacob's face. He let go of my wrist and I staggered backwards.

"I suppose you think he's better than me," he said, "just because he can read and write and do those fancy drawings. My horseshoe weren't good enough for you, were it? Dumped it on the ground, didn't you? But you'll run about after him when he shows you an old snail. Well, you want to watch out. People will start to talk, and you'll be out on your ear with no character. And who will have you then?"

"Mind your own business, Jacob," I said. "What I do in my own time has nothing to do with you."

I turned and marched into the house. I could feel his eyes on my back as I walked away, and I hoped he couldn't see my hands trembling.

CHAPTER TWENTY-ONE

A Refusal

My head throbbed and my stomach churned as I went about my tasks that evening. Had Charles Ellerdale come to propose to Sophia? Was she about to refuse him and be locked up before she had a chance to escape?

I listened at the door of the White Parlour, but I couldn't hear anything. I tried to get information out of George, who had been waiting at the table during dinner, but he had nothing of interest to say. Surely that was a good sign? Oh, I hoped so.

After supper, I was filling the coal scuttle in Mrs Bailey's dressing room when I heard the crunch of hooves on gravel. I hurried to the window. Through the dusk, I saw Charles Ellerdale's carriage tearing away up the drive.

What did that mean? Had he proposed and been turned down? Or had he not proposed tonight? My heart was thumping. I couldn't stand this much longer.

The stable clock struck nine as I crossed the cobbles to empty Mrs Bailey's chamber pot. An owl hooted nearby and another owl, deeper in the woods, replied. With my face turned away, I tipped the contents of the pot on the dung heap and walked back towards the house. Then my heart stopped as I saw Sophia, ghostly in the moonlight, slipping across the deserted stable yard. Was she on her way to meet Robbie?

And then I saw something that filled me with joy. She was carrying a bag.

I wanted to skip and shout and dance. They were running away! They *did* have a plan, and it was the right plan! They were leaving Charlbury and I could go back to the twenty-first century. The wonderful, amazing twenty-first century, with taps and toilets and TV and wifi. And my own home, with my own mum.

My warnings had worked. I couldn't believe it. I felt dizzy with happiness.

I crept the rest of the way out of the woods, terrified that Sophia might see me and think I was spying. But I made it safely to the edge of the wood and was walking through the passage between the buildings, about to step out on to the cobbles, when a shout shattered the silence.

"Sophia! Come here this instant, I command you!"

Sir Henry pounded into the stable yard, sending rooks cawing and wheeling into the sky.

My heart stopped. What would Sophia do? I ran to the other end of the passage.

Sophia dashed into the wood. Her white dress billowed around her as she darted through the trees, the gossamer-thin fabric translucent in the moonlight.

Then she stumbled and cried out. Her foot seemed to be caught in the undergrowth. She struggled to disentangle herself but one of her dainty evening shoes came off. She crammed it back on her foot.

"Get back here, you brazen little hussy!" bellowed Sir Henry.

Sophia ran further into the woods but her dress snagged on a patch of brambles. She tugged at the fabric.

From the stable yard, I heard Mrs Bailey's voice. "Sir Henry," she said in a voice much quieter than her brother's, but deadly with anger, "have you completely forgotten yourself? Remember the servants, for goodness' sake, and keep yourself under control."

"Hang the servants!" he shouted, crashing through the trees towards his daughter. Sophia, her dress now caught in several places, hurled her bag into the undergrowth. Sir Henry reached her, tangled in the thorns, and grabbed her arm. She tried to shake it off but he yanked her towards him.

"Come back to the house this instant, do you hear me?" His voice trembled with anger.

Sophia lifted her face to look him in the eye and drew herself up very straight and tall.

"Very well, Father."

I slid down the rough brick wall of the passage until I was sitting on the ground, my head in my hands. So this was it. He was going to lock her up, and I would never get back to the present.

I looked up to see Sophia tearing her dress away from the brambles, leaving little pieces of fabric attached to the thorns. She seemed to have completely given up the fight. She allowed her father to escort her back to the stable yard, as meek as a beaten spaniel. I forced myself to get up and tiptoe to the other end of the dark passage, where the three of them now stood only a few metres from where I was pressed against the cold wall. I could see them all in profile in the moonlight, Sophia facing the other two across the cobbles.

"Come indoors, Sophia," said Mrs Bailey in an icy voice, "and stop making a spectacle of yourself. Look at your gown, torn to pieces."

"I want nothing to do with this gown," said Sophia. "I want nothing to do with any of it." She gestured at the house, her dress, the stable yard. "Every inch of it is tainted. It sickens me."

Mrs Bailey threw a meaningful glance at Sir Henry. "She has gone mad. I suspected as much."

Sir Henry stepped forward and shook Sophia roughly by the shoulders.

"I want the truth and I want it now. Why, after he spoke to you in the White Parlour, did Charles Ellerdale leave the house in a tearing hurry with a face like a thunderstorm? Why did you come running out here in this lunatic fashion? Tell me exactly what occurred between you or I shall whip you to within an inch of your life. Good God, to be so shamed in my own house!"

Sophia took a deep breath and looked her father

in the eye.

"Sir, I know that Mr Ellerdale asked you for my hand in marriage this evening."

"Did he propose to you? If he spoke, and you refused him—"

"He has not yet asked me to marry him," said Sophia. "But he strongly hinted that he would do so tomorrow night. I must inform you, sir, that when he does, I shall refuse him."

Mrs Bailey gasped. I banged my forehead on the wall in despair. What was she doing? Did she *want* to be locked up?

"*Refuse!*" shouted Sir Henry. "You little... *Refuse* Charles Ellerdale, with a thousand acres and a palace of a house? What right do you think you have, you little wretch, to refuse such a man? Why, you—"

"Do you know where his money came from?" said Sophia. "Oh, he told me. Boasted of it, indeed. So proud he is, of his trade in human lives. His ships, sailing out to Africa, loaded with guns and ironware, to be traded for people – people! – packed into the hold and shipped to the West Indies, and traded there, like merchandise, for sugar."

"And what of it?" said her father. "The sugar plantations need labour. Where do you think you would get your tea and coffee from, your silks and cottons, if not from the colonies?"

"Exactly," said Sophia. "It is all tainted. Now that I know by what means it was obtained, I want nothing more to do with any of it."

Her father gave a scornful laugh. "And you'll

wear worsted, spun with your own hands, and eat potatoes you've grown yourself, will you, and live in a hovel like a peasant?"

"I simply think, sir," said Sophia, "that we ought to treat people with dignity and respect. After all, it is a mere accident of birth that we were born into privilege and others into poverty. It is not right – it cannot be right – for a person to buy and sell another person."

"I knew it," said Mrs Bailey. "She has lost her mind. Spouting ridiculous, revolutionary ideas, just like her mother."

Sophia wheeled round to face her aunt.

"Do not *ever* speak of my mother in that way. I assure you that I am of perfectly sound mind, as was my mother. It is simply that I have been reading and thinking about the world."

"Ha!" barked her father. "Reading! Thinking! I should have stopped that nonsense long ago. This is what happens when we teach women to read."

"I have lived my life in luxury and ignorance," said Sophia. "Never before did it occur to me to wonder where my food came from, who spun the silk for my gowns, who crawled underground to mine the coal for my fires, who swept my chimneys. But now I know, and I am ashamed. All these things are done by people. People just like us, had we not had the fortune to be born into wealth."

Her father snorted. "What utter drivel! Do you want to see the streets of London running with blood? Because that's what happens when people start to interfere with the God-given order of society. Look at France. Is that what you want here? You'd be the first to the guillotine, do you realise that? But you don't hear the servants here complaining about their lot in life, do you? Some are born to govern and some to serve. That's how the world works, and God help us if people forget it. Do you really think the country would be a better place if it were ruled by drunken footmen and imbecilic housemaids?"

"I think there should be more equality and respect between the social classes, that is all," said Sophia. "It cannot be right to treat human beings as commodities, to be bought and sold."

"Someone has been filling her head with this stuff," said her aunt, taking a step closer to Sophia. "Who is it?"

"I have been talking to people," said Sophia. "And I have discovered terrible things. Did you know that in this very village there are children, some as young as four, torn from their beds every day to spin silk in a factory, from five in the morning until six at night? Work for which they are paid less than twopence per day. And in these fields – *your* fields, sir – there are young boys working all day long, in all weathers, for no reward but beatings and starvation."

Sir Henry stepped forward and grasped her shoulders.

"Who has been feeding you this nonsense?"

Sophia suddenly looked frightened. "I... I read it," she stuttered. "In a pamphlet."

"Nonsense. There are no radical pamphlets in this

house. You are lying. You said you had been talking to people. I demand to know who has put these ideas in your head."

"No."

A sudden clap of thunder made me jump.

"No?" repeated Sir Henry, incredulously.

"No. I shall not tell you, and I shall not marry Charles Ellerdale. I shall marry for love or not at all, and that is final."

"Marry for love?" he barked. "Marry for *love*? Is this what I brought you up for, educated you for, gave you every luxury and accomplishment for? Do you know how much you have cost me? Do you know how much this house costs to run? Why, you ungrateful young baggage, you—"

He raised his arm, but Mrs Bailey grabbed it. "Not in public, sir," she hissed.

I felt a drop of water on my arm. Rain started splashing on the cobblestones.

Sir Henry swatted his sister's hand away and took a step closer to Sophia. "You shall do your duty to your family and marry Charles Ellerdale," he said, through clenched teeth, "or I shall whip you into obedience."

"You can whip me to death," Sophia said, "but I shall never marry Charles Ellerdale."

The rain was falling harder now, bouncing off the cobblestones and soaking through my dress.

"Bring me my whip," barked Sir Henry to his sister.

"Sir Henry," said Mrs Bailey, "think before you

act, for heaven's sake. Will Charles Ellerdale want a girl who bears the scars of your whip on her back?"

"Are you telling me she should not be punished?"

"Of course she must be punished. But I think not with a whip."

"So what do you suggest?" he snapped.

"For now, sir, I would suggest you lock her in her room. Perhaps some time alone will help her understand her duty to her family."

He hesitated. Then he said, "Very well."

Suddenly Sophia bolted across the yard. Sir Henry gave a roar of fury and bounded after her. She stumbled and her shoe came off again. Her father grabbed her by the arm and dragged her back across the cobbles.

"You can lock me away for the rest of my life," she said, "but you will never change my mind."

"Why, you stubborn, insolent little—"

He walloped her around the head.

Before I knew what I was doing, I ran into the yard. Somehow I had to stop her from being locked up.

"Hey!" I yelled. Maybe I could distract Sir Henry and give Sophia the chance to get away.

But he didn't even turn round. He marched her towards the front door, her aunt following.

The side door opened. Light spilled across the cobbles.

"Evie!" called Polly. "Are you out there? Evie, come in."

I carried on running after Sir Henry. "Hey!" I

yelled again. But Polly caught up with me, grabbed my arm and pulled me towards the scullery door.

"Get off!" I shouted, trying to wrench her hand away. "I have to stop him. Get off me."

But Polly had my arm in an iron grip. "Oh, Evie," she gasped, pulling me towards the house. "Evie, there is such a commotion inside."

"What? What's happened?"

"Alice is dying!"

"Dying?" I stared at her, horrified.

"And... Oh, Evie..." Polly looked at me with huge, frightened eyes. "She says... She says you have killed her."

CHAPTER TWENTY-TWO

Witchcraft

I stared at Polly, uncomprehending. "*Killed* her? What do you mean?"

Polly started to speak but at that moment Mrs Hardwick appeared and gave me a tremendous slap across the side of the face. I cried out and staggered sideways.

"Get off me!" I yelled, beside myself now. "Will you just stop hitting me!"

She responded by gripping my shoulders and shaking me. "Ever since you arrived in this house, young lady, you've been nothing but trouble. And now you send the kitchen maid into hysterics and turn the household into chaos. I tell you—"

"What are you talking about? What have I done? I haven't done anything to Alice."

Mrs Hardwick snorted. "Well, she's writhing on her bed, screaming in agony, in such a state that no one can get near, saying you've bewitched her."

"*Bewitched* her?"

"You surely don't believe that, missus," said Polly. "Alice is just saying it because she hates Evie."

"Witchcraft or no witchcraft," said Mrs Hardwick,

"I'll put up with it no longer. Fetch your box and leave this instant."

I turned cold with dread. "What? No!"

I couldn't leave the house. I just couldn't. If I wasn't at Charlbury, how would I ever find my way home?

Mrs Hardwick raised her arm again. "You'll do what I tell you, missy, and none of your chat."

"You can hit me all you like but I'm not going."

"Oh, please, missus," said Polly, "have some mercy. You can't send her away at night, into the rain, with nowhere to go."

But Mrs Hardwick gave me a look that showed no mercy. "Get up to your room and fetch your things. I want you out of this house in five minutes flat."

I almost told her I had no things, but then I realised that going up to the attic would at least give me the chance to talk to Polly, and I shut my mouth.

"Polly, I have to stay," I said as we walked up the back stairs. "I can't leave this house."

"I wish you could," she said, "but I know Hardwitch. Once her mind's made up, there's nothing anybody can do to change it."

I wished I could tell Polly everything. I wished I could tell her that my real life was two hundred years in the future, and that the only way I knew how to get back to that life was through the magic in this house. But if I said that to Polly, then she would think I was a witch too.

But I had to stay here. I had to help Sophia escape and I had to get back to my own time.

Even before we reached the attic corridor, I could hear Alice's hysterical sobbing.

"Do you think she's really dying?" I asked Polly.

"I don't know. I would have said she's putting it on to get rid of you, but that's quite a performance if it's not real."

I marched down the corridor and knocked on Alice's door. The moaning and wailing continued. I knocked harder but there was still no answer.

"Alice," I called. "It's me. Evie. Let me in. I need to talk to you."

Alice screamed.

I tried to open the door but it was locked. I pleaded again through the keyhole but she screamed even more hysterically. I turned to Polly in despair. "I don't understand. How can she be dying when she was perfectly fine a couple of hours ago?"

"I've no idea," Polly said, "but if you value your life you'd better get away as quickly as you can."

I stared at her. "What do you mean? Nobody will really believe I bewitched her, will they?"

Polly looked uncomfortable. "She says she saw you gathering herbs and muttering to yourself."

"What?" I slipped my hand in my pocket and felt the limp leaves. "I did pick herbs. They smelled nice." The meaning of Polly's words dawned on me and I laughed at the sheer craziness of it. "Is she saying I was making a *potion* or something?"

"She says you've poisoned her. And she says she's seen three portents of death since you came here."

"Portents of *death*?"

190

"She says a coal flew out of the fire and landed at her feet in the shape of a coffin."

"And she thinks that's a sign of death?"

"And then she said the tallow rose up the wick of her candle that night, which is supposed to foretell a death in the family. And when the chimney sweep's dog howled while we were at breakfast, that was the third portent."

"But surely people don't really believe that stuff?"

"I don't. But some do."

I remembered Mary, Betty and Alice huddled together in the servants' hall, shushing each other as I came in. Then I thought of the malicious looks Alice was always giving me, and of how she jogged my elbow and kicked my sweepings down the stairs.

"I don't think Alice believes it herself," I said. "She's just saying it to get me in trouble. She wants me out of here. And she's succeeded."

From along the corridor, Alice gave a particularly piercing scream.

"Or maybe she actually is ill," I said, "and she thinks blaming me is a good way to get me sacked. Then she can work with you, like she's always wanted."

"But where will you go, Evie? What will you do?"

"I'm not going," I said, panic rising inside me. "I can't. Polly, you've got to help me. Persuade Mrs Hardwick to let me stay. I can't leave. I've got nothing."

Polly's face was full of concern. "I wish I could," she said, "but I won't be able to change her mind.

She never budges once her mind's set on a thing. But you could try to get work in the silk factory in the village. And the weather's not too cold, at least. That's a blessing. It won't be so bad if you have to sleep out for a while, until you get your first wages and you can find lodgings."

I stared at Polly, speechless. I couldn't believe this was actually happening.

The door at the end of the corridor opened, and Nell came scampering along the passage.

"Excuse me," she said, not meeting my eye, "but Mrs Hardwick says you're to be out of the house in five minutes flat or she'll have you whipped."

"You must go, Evie," said Polly with fear in her eyes. "They hang folks for poisoning." She put a hand in the small of my back and hurried me down the corridor, Nell scuttling behind us. I felt numb.

"I shall miss you," Polly said. "Write to me if you get the chance. I'll get George to read it to me. I've never had a letter."

CHAPTER TWENTY-THREE

Shut Out

In the basement hall, George was shrugging off his jacket. His camp bed lay across the doorway.

"Sorry to hear you're leaving," he said. "Bad business, that." He pushed the bed aside and slid back the bolts. "When you get to the gates, knock on the lodgekeeper's door. He'll open up for you."

He shut the door behind me and I heard the bolts being drawn across.

It was pitch dark. The rain had stopped and water dripped from the roofs and the trees. I walked slowly up the drive, wondering how I was able even to put one foot in front of the other. I had no money, no spare clothes, not a single possession. And outside these gates, I didn't know a soul in this world.

I felt hollow inside. An outline of a person, with no substance. A ghost of my former self. My past was in another world and I was walking towards an unknown future.

I turned to take one last look back at the moonlit house. Most of the windows were in darkness or had their curtains drawn so that only a few chinks of light were visible at the edges. But there was one window on the second floor that had no curtain drawn across it. A candlelit figure stood at the window. A figure in a white nightdress, with long dark hair. Sophia, locked in her room.

I had failed to help her and now I was trapped in the past. How was I ever going to get back?

The lodgekeeper shut the gate behind me and I squelched along the muddy track. Was I the only person ever to have travelled in time, I wondered, or were there other people like me in the world? Other lost and lonely time travellers who couldn't tell anybody what was happening to them because they would be thought crazy?

Overwhelmed with misery, I trudged on towards the village. The only option seemed to be to beg for work in the silk factory. But how long would it be before I got paid? How would I buy food until then? Where would I sleep? And what if I couldn't get a job at all? Would I end up in the workhouse?

Through the fog of despair in my head, I gradually became aware of the thud and splash of hooves behind me. I turned, and recognised the rider. It was George.

"Evie!" he called.

He drew level with me and brought the horse to a stop. "I've been sent to fetch you. Hop up behind me. You're to come back to Charlbury."

My insides leapt with hope, then contracted with terror. "Why? Who sent you? Why do they want me back?"

Was I going to be whipped? Or even … hanged?

If I bolted through the hedge and ran into those woods, would I have a chance of escape?

"Hardwitch sent me," said George. "And don't try to make a run for it," he added, reading my thoughts. "I'm a champion runner, and Rufus here ain't bad either. Come on, put your foot in that stirrup and I'll give you a hand up."

He took my hand in a firm grip. I had no choice.

"Why has she sent for me?" I asked, scrambling on to the horse's back.

"Put your arms round me and hold on," said George, flicking the reins. "I don't know why. That was all she said – 'Go and fetch Evie back'. I know better than to question Hardwitch."

"But how did she say it? Did she sound angry?"

"As angry as she generally does. Now quit asking me questions."

So the questions buzzed around my head instead. Horrible, terrifying questions. Had Alice died? Would I be arrested for murder?

Back at the house, George handed me over to William's charge. William led me up the back stairs and knocked on the door of the housekeeper's room. I felt as though my insides were dissolving.

Mrs Hardwick was standing by the fireplace, her face grim, her body rigid. Mrs Winter sat at the table, glaring at me, her enormous backside spilling over the edges of a dining chair.

I gripped the back of a chair for support.

"You may go, William," said Mrs Hardwick.

William left the room. The housekeeper cleared

her throat. I realised I was shivering.

"Evie," said Mrs Hardwick, "it appears that there has been a misunderstanding."

She paused. I tried to stop shivering, but I couldn't. She cleared her throat again. She looked uncomfortable.

"Alice is not dying," she said. "She thought she was dying, but in fact she has merely started her monthlies. It appears she had no idea what to expect."

Her monthlies?

Oh. Her periods.

"The stupid girl convinced herself she was at death's door. And it seems she had taken a dislike to you for some reason and had been spreading rumours that you were practising witchcraft."

There was a knock at the door.

"Come in," said Mrs Hardwick.

The door opened. Polly was standing there with Alice, whose head was lowered so much that I couldn't see her expression.

"Here's Alice to see you, missus," said Polly, and as she turned to go, she gave me a broad smile and a wink. A huge weight lifted from my shoulders. If Polly was grinning like that, then things must be all right. I felt weak with relief. My legs buckled. If I hadn't been gripping the back of the chair, I would have collapsed.

Alice shuffled into the room, her head down.

"Well, what have you got to say to Evie?" demanded Mrs Hardwick.

"I am very sorry," muttered Alice, her eyes fixed on the floor.

"I should think so," snapped Mrs Winter, suddenly coming to venomous life. "Of all the stupid, hysterical, dim-witted kitchen maids I have ever had the misfortune to be saddled with, you are the very worst. Now, pack your bags and go."

Alice gave the cook a single miserable look, then turned without a word. "Oh, please don't sack her," I burst out.

Alice wheeled round and stared at me, her eyes huge with amazement.

Mrs Hardwick gave me an incredulous look. "Don't be ridiculous. I certainly can't have the pair of you working together, so one of you will have to go."

"Mrs Hardwick, Mrs Winter, please let Alice stay. It was just a misunderstanding. Alice knows now that I don't mean her any harm, don't you, Alice? We'll both get on with our jobs and we won't cause you any more trouble."

Alice's mouth gaped open and her eyes were wide with wonder.

Mrs Hardwick sighed with impatience. She turned to the cook. "What is your opinion, Mrs Winter?"

Mrs Winter huffed. "She's a lazy useless slattern, but every kitchen maid I've ever had is a lazy useless slattern, and at least she's trained up. I suppose it beats training up another."

Mrs Hardwick glared at me, at Alice and at Mrs Winter. Then she gave an exasperated sigh. "Very well then, Alice, you may stay. But this incident will never be mentioned again. There will be no gossiping and no rumour-mongering, do you hear me? If I have another shred of trouble from either of you, you'll be straight out without a backward glance. Is that clear?"

"Yes, missus," we chorused.

"Now, get to bed, the pair of you. We've wasted quite enough time on this ridiculous business as it is."

"That was good of you, to want her to stay," said Polly as she took out her hairpins.

I sat on the bed to unlace my boots. "I just felt so sorry for her. Imagine how scary it must have been, to start bleeding and have no idea what was happening. I looked at her standing in front of that mean old cook, and I just thought how lonely and miserable she must be. And imagine being thrown out of here and having nowhere to go. I mean, it nearly happened to me, and I know how horrible it feels. I wouldn't want it to happen to anyone else."

"Well, it was very kind of you. It is pretty miserable for her here, but at least she gets her bed and board. She could have it a lot worse."

As I sank into bed, I was overwhelmed with relief. I was back at Charlbury!

But was I just kidding myself, to imagine that I could help Sophia escape? Tomorrow would be the twenty-seventh of April, the date scratched into the glass. Sophia had been locked up for the rest of her life. Was it really possible to change the past?

But if it wasn't, then why was I here?

Then, like a blow to the chest, a terrible thought struck me. Could this be some horrific supernatural punishment because I'd been so horrible to Mum lately? Anna had said these things were passed down in families. Would I be separated from Mum forever, just as she had been separated from her mother, and Sophia's child had been separated from her?

CHAPTER TWENTY-FOUR

The Plan

When I woke up it was still pitch dark. But even though I couldn't see anything, I could tell I was still in the attic room with Polly, in 1814.

I closed my eyes and lay motionless, feeling so heavy with hopelessness that I didn't think I would ever be able to move again.

Polly, whose internal alarm clock never seemed to fail, sprang upright in bed as the stable clock struck five.

"Up you get, Evie."

I opened my eyes to see her smiling at me. "I'm proper glad that business with Alice was sorted out," she said. "You're a shocking housemaid, but at least I shan't be working alone all day. You can teach me to read some more too."

And as she spoke I found myself, to my complete surprise, filled with a sudden surge of determination. I had promised to help Sophia, so that was what I must do. If there was any hope at all of getting back to my own life, in my own time, I was going to have to sort out this situation. Everything about it was strange and terrifying, not to mention completely barking mad, but, as far as I could see, there was only one hope, and that was to get Sophia and Robbie out of here and give their story a happy ending.

How was I going to do it though? I couldn't put a foot out of line, that much was clear. Mrs Hardwick wasn't going to give me any more chances, and there was no way I was going to risk being thrown out of the house again. So I would have to act the part of the perfect housemaid, while coming up with a foolproof plan to help Sophia escape.

All I needed now was a foolproof plan.

When Polly and I walked into the servants' hall for breakfast, everybody else was already at the table. The girls looked at me curiously, but nobody said anything. I wondered if Mrs Hardwick had had a word with them.

As we sat down, Alice walked in through the other door, carrying a wooden tray laid with a white linen cloth. On the cloth stood a teapot, a cup and saucer and two slices of bread on a plate. Alice set the tray down at the end of the long table.

"You're to take this to Miss Fane's room, Polly," she said, keeping her eyes on the tray.

"Is that all she's having?" asked Polly, as Alice left the room.

"Mrs Bailey's orders," said Mrs Hardwick. She took a key from the bunch at her waist and placed it on the tray. "Unlock the door with this, place the tray just inside the room and leave immediately, locking the door behind you. Return the key to me."

"What about cleaning her room?"

"Nobody is to enter for any purpose but to take and collect trays and chamber pots," said Mrs Hardwick, rising from the table and smoothing down her skirts. "Mrs Bailey's orders."

As soon as she closed the door behind her, George raised his eyebrows. "Dry bread with the door locked? What's Miss Fane gone and done now?"

"I did hear shouting last evening," said Polly. "In the stable yard, it was. I thought the master was shouting at one of the stable boys, but then I heard women's voices, and I thought that was odd. You was out there, Evie. Didn't you hear anything?"

I shook my head, my eyes fixed on the tablecloth. "Not really."

"Mr Ellerdale," said William, "was speaking to Miss Fane after dinner in the White Parlour, private-like, and all of a sudden he jumps up and takes his leave, all offended-like. And Miss Fane rushes off too, in a big hurry, and then the master jumps up and runs off after her."

He took a big bite of his bread and a swig of beer. Everyone was looking at him.

"And then what?" said Mary.

"Eh?" he asked with his mouth full.

"What happened next?"

"How should I know? I were clearing dishes, weren't I?"

Mary sighed with exasperation.

"The master was hitting the whisky bottle pretty hard last night, I know that," said George. "Kept ringing the bell for more. In a filthy temper, he was."

"So Miss Fane has upset Mr Ellerdale," said Betty. "Refused his hand, I expect. And who can blame her?"

The door opened and we all concentrated on breakfast. Mrs Hardwick swept her laser eyes around the table.

"I'd advise you all to keep your mouths shut and avoid peddling tittle-tattle about your betters, unless you want to find yourselves in the poorhouse sharpish. Have you not taken that tray to Miss Fane, Polly? Stir yourself, for goodness' sake."

I jumped up. "I'll do it."

"Steady on," said William. "You nearly spilled my beer."

Polly looked at me curiously. "What's got into you all of a sudden?"

"Nothing," I said. "But you've been on your feet all morning, Polly. Sit and finish your breakfast."

I took the tray and walked upstairs as slowly as I dared, trying to give myself some thinking time.

Sophia was lying on her four-poster bed, staring at the ceiling. She didn't move when I came in.

I set the tray down on the table. "Your breakfast, Miss Fane."

At the sound of my voice, she turned her head sharply.

"You?" she said, glaring at me. Then all the energy left her face. She turned her head to the opposite wall and sighed.

I took that as a good sign. At least she hadn't

thrown me out. Not yet anyway.

"How are you, Miss Fane?"

"I am kept a prisoner in my own house by my father and my aunt," snapped Sophia, "so how do you imagine I am?"

Fair enough. It was a stupid question.

"You have to escape," I said. "You have to get away with Robbie."

"Shh!" she said, springing out of bed and grasping my shoulders, a look of terror on her face that instantly turned to fury. "Do you wish to get us both killed?"

"Sorry, sorry," I said. "Do you mind not gripping my shoulders? It really hurts."

Sophia's eyes were darting around the room, as though she was expecting spies to jump out of the wardrobe.

"I won't mention his name again," I whispered. Then, as she continued to grip my shoulder, "It's fine, honestly. I was speaking really quietly and there's no one else around."

Finally she relaxed her grip. She sat down heavily on the bed, frowning intensely at me, as though trying to find the answer to a puzzle.

"Who are you?" she asked eventually. "You foretold what would happen, and you seem to wish to help me. Why? What is your motive?"

Perhaps, I thought, she would be more likely to believe me if she thought I wasn't just a random housemaid. It was worth a try anyway.

"I had a dream," I said. "You appeared at my

window in a dream, and you asked me to help you."

She stared at me for an uncomfortably long time, and I couldn't read her expression. Finally she said, "What is your name?"

"Evie, ma'am."

She was silent for a while. Then she gave a sad little laugh.

"Well, Evie," she said, "I suppose I have nothing to lose. I am already locked in my room. And there is nobody else."

"So you'll let me help you escape?"

She sighed impatiently. "How can I escape? It is impossible. If I go in daylight, I will certainly be stopped, and there is no means of leaving Charlbury at night. Every door and window is locked and bolted."

"Then you must leave at dusk," I said, "just before the house is locked."

She gave a bitter laugh. "I tried that last night, and look where I am now."

"Yes, but you've got to be smarter in the way you do it. You mustn't anger your father. If you'd been charming and sweet to Mr Ellerdale at dinner, and then you'd just said you needed some air and you were going outside for a moment, no one would have suspected anything and you could have got safely away before they realised."

"It is all very well saying that after the event," she snapped. "What use is your advice to me now I am locked up?"

But my mind was working fast for once. "Your

father and your aunt said you'll be locked up until you agree to marry Mr Ellerdale, is that right?"

"Gracious, gossip does travel quickly. I suppose the entire staff knows everything by now."

"So you must agree to marry Mr Ellerdale."

Sophia looked furious. "I shall die in this room before I agree to marry that man."

"I'm not saying you should marry him. I'm saying you should tell your father you will marry him. Beg your father's forgiveness for your crazy behaviour last night. Tell him you temporarily lost your senses, but now you have seen the error of your ways and you realise that your duty is to your family and your father. Then this evening you can have dinner as usual, acting the perfect, obedient daughter. And at nine o'clock – that should be a good time, while the servants are having supper and the house is still unlocked – at nine o'clock you smile sweetly and ask to be excused for a second. And then you leave the house, meet Robbie and get away as quickly as you can."

Sophia stared at me in silence for a few seconds, her eyes huge. Then she stood up and started to pace the room.

"That might work," she murmured. "It might actually work." She walked up and down the room in silence for a few more minutes, and then she turned to me. "Could you ask a footman to take a message to my father, asking to speak with him in the library? I shall ask him to explain to Mr Ellerdale that I was simply overawed by the attentions of such a distinguished gentleman, but now that I have had time to recover my composure, I should be delighted and grateful to receive him."

"That's perfect," I said. "He'll be overjoyed."

Sophia's eyes were alight with excitement now. "We have been planning this for weeks. We shall walk overnight to Lower Mistleham. From there, Robbie says there is a stagecoach to London that departs very early in the morning. In London, Robbie says, we may melt into a crowd and nobody will know us. And from there we shall take stagecoaches all the way to Scotland, and then we shall be married!"

"Scotland? Why don't you get married in London?"

Sophia looked at me as though I was completely stupid. "Why, because the law is different in Scotland, of course. We can marry there without my father's consent. We can be married at Gretna Green, as soon as we cross the border." She flopped down on the bed with a blissful sigh. "Married! Oh, Evie, it is as though I have known him all my life. We are kindred souls. We have read the same books, we admire the same poets, we believe the same things about how the world should be changed." She was speaking very fast now, the words pouring out of her in a torrent. It seemed that, now I had come up with an idea she liked, she had finally decided to trust me. "Is it not strange? Our backgrounds so different and yet we think so alike. He has the most wonderful ideas. And his drawings! His drawings are extraordinary. He is the most talented man I have ever met. And yet, my father—"

The landing door banged and footsteps sounded in the corridor.

"I must go," I whispered. "I was told to bring the tray and leave immediately. I'll find Robbie during my break. Where should I tell him to meet you?"

"In the orchard. We shall leave by the back gate, across the fields."

The footsteps were very close now. I nodded, left the room and fastened all the locks and bolts. Madame Perrault passed the door without even looking at me. She had a face on her as though somebody was holding a rotting carcass to her nose.

As soon as she had passed me, I gave an enormous grin and had to stop myself from skipping down the corridor. I couldn't believe what had just happened. It had gone better than I had dared to hope. And if Sophia played her part well with her father and Charles Ellerdale this evening, there was no reason why she wouldn't be able to run away with Robbie tonight.

And if they got away successfully, then... Oh, please let it be true... Then maybe ... if the time travel really did work in the way I thought it did ... then I would wake up tomorrow in Anna's flat, back in the twenty-first century.

CHAPTER TWENTY-FIVE

A Threat

George appeared in the doorway of the servants' hall as the rest of us were sitting down for lunch.

"If Mr Paxton asks for me," he said, "tell him I have to ride over to Mr Ellerdale's with a message."

"Oh, yes?" said Mary. "What's the message?"

George held up a piece of paper, folded and sealed with wax. "Let's just say I shouldn't be surprised if Miss Fane has changed her mind about Mr Ellerdale. The master's in remarkably high spirits and I was told to ride over and deliver this immediately. So I've no time to stand around gossiping with you lot."

As the others broke out in excited chatter, I turned away to hide my delight.

The first part of the plan had worked.

During our break Polly and I went to the farmyard behind the stable block and found a few lumps of chalk and a broken plank, which would do instead of a slate for the time being. She was a quick learner and it didn't take long before she could read and write the sentence 'Polly is a cat and dog'. It didn't make a lot of sense, but it used all her new words.

Polly was so excited by this that I was worried she would want to use the whole hour and I wouldn't get the chance to tell Robbie to meet Sophia in the orchard at nine o'clock. I was trying to think of an excuse to go off alone when Polly started yawning.

"I'm going for a quick doss down," she said. "Coming?"

"Thanks, but I feel like a walk," I said.

It seemed to be my lucky day, because I found Robbie in the first place I looked. He was weeding a vegetable bed at the end of the kitchen garden, by the shed. To add to my luck, he seemed to be alone again. I couldn't believe how well this was all working out.

As I walked towards him, along the grassy paths between the neat rows of vegetables, he put his finger to his lips and pointed to a shelf just inside the shed, to the right of the open door.

The inside of the tool shed was dark, and at first I couldn't tell what I was supposed to be looking at. There was a ball of twine on the shelf, and some empty plant pots.

And then I saw it, and drew in my breath. A neat little nest of twigs and hay and, poking out of the top of it, three huge yellow beaks, gaping open.

I turned, wide-eyed, to Robbie. "Wow," I mouthed.

He smiled, and then he pointed to a plump robin perched on the garden wall. It looked at us with its shiny black eyes, and then looked at the ground. It seemed to be considering.

We waited, motionless.

Suddenly the robin opened its wings and flew down on to the freshly turned earth beside Robbie's fork. It plucked a long slimy worm from the soil and immediately flew up again, the worm clamped in its beak. It flew into the shed, perched on the edge of the nest and stuffed the wriggling worm into one of the chicks' huge open beaks. I watched, fascinated.

"They do that all day long," said Robbie in a low voice. "Both parents, backwards and forwards, feeding those chicks."

"But they're so tiny," I said. "How can they need so much food?"

"They leave the nest at two weeks old. So they have a lot of growing to do in a fortnight."

"Two weeks!"

"Yep. And then they're all alone in the world."

Something in his tone made me turn to him. There was a look of deep sadness in his eyes.

I looked around the garden again to check we were alone. Then I said in a low voice, "Sophia has told her father she will marry Mr Ellerdale."

He gave an anguished moan and clasped his head in his hands. I stepped forward and touched his arm.

"You don't have to worry," I said. "She's not actually going to marry him." And I told him the rest of the plan.

It was amazing to watch his mood change from despair to ecstasy in a matter of seconds. By the end of my explanation, he was gazing at me as though I was some sort of god. And I suppose I almost was. I mean, not to boast or anything, but it isn't everyone who actually gets to change the course of history.

"Why are you doing so much to help us, Evie?" he said. "Why do you care so much?"

I wished that I could tell the truth. It would have been such a relief to tell him the real story. But I couldn't risk it. He would think I was either a lunatic or a witch, and who could blame him? And I really needed him to trust my sanity. So I just said, "I can't bear to think of Soph— Miss Fane – being locked up for the rest of her life, that's all. I haven't really done much."

"You have done everything," he said. "We can never repay you for your kindness."

"You don't need to repay me," I said. "Just make sure you get away safely."

At five o'clock I went down to the kitchen to fill the hot water cans for the dressing rooms. Mrs Winter was making pastry at one end of the table, while Alice chopped onions at the other. Judging by the clatter coming from the scullery, Nell was washing dishes.

Suddenly the door opened and Mrs Bailey swept in. It was hard to curtsey while holding a water can under a hot tap but I managed an awkward bob. Not that Mrs Bailey so much as glanced in my direction.

"We are expecting Mr Ellerdale for dinner tonight," she said to the cook.

"Very good, madam."

"It will need to be a special dinner. We are expecting it to be something of a celebration."

"Very good, madam," said Mrs Winter.

That godlike feeling came over me again. I felt as though I was directing a play, and all my actors were playing their parts to perfection. Only a few more hours now until Robbie and Sophia would be safely away from here and I would be back in my own time.

If that was how the time travel worked, said the little voice of doubt in my head.

Be quiet, I told the voice.

Later, as I crossed the stable yard with Sir Henry's chamber pot, Jacob emerged from a stable and swaggered towards me with a smirk on his face. I had a funny feeling he was waiting for me. Waiting to pounce.

"Did you have a pleasant conversation earlier?" he asked in a strange, affected voice.

"Conversation?"

"I had a little stroll in the orchard a while ago," he said in the same fake voice. "Delightful place for a stroll, the orchard. And it's funny, sometimes, what a person can accidentally overhear during an innocent walk."

My stomach lurched. When I had spoken to Robbie, we were standing only centimetres away from the wall that bordered the orchard. Had Jacob been listening on the other side of that wall? How much had he heard?

My brain worked frantically. It would be no good to demand to know what he had heard. He would only tell me what he wanted me to know. Could I plead with him, or would that make things worse? Was there anything I could do?

A triumphant look came over his face. Too late, I realised I shouldn't have shown my panic.

I fixed my eyes on a tree in the wood. "I don't know what you're talking about," I said, trying to sound bored and uninterested.

"I should think," said Jacob, "that Sir Henry would be *very* interested in what I have to tell him."

I felt sick. I refused to meet his eye but I could feel him looking at me intently, as if trying to gauge my response.

"Unless, of course," he continued, "*unless* something happens to drive the conversation out of my mind."

"What are you talking about?" I said, loathing him more every second.

He grabbed my shoulders.

"Get off me!" I pulled away, but he tightened his grip.

"Kiss me," he demanded.

"*What?!* Get *off*!"

He pulled me to him, one hand on the back of my head and the other around my waist. Still holding the chamber pot in one hand, I fought to get out of his grasp but it was useless: he was far too strong. I screwed my eyes shut and clamped my lips together, trying to push away his rough mouth against mine, the stink of garlic and onions and rotten breath, the scratching of his stubbly chin. I felt as though I was going to throw up.

"Evie! Get inside the house this instant!"

Jacob shoved me away and, without a backward glance, turned and walked into the stable block.

I turned round, grimacing and frantically wiping my mouth on my sleeve. The bony figure of Mrs Hardwick loomed in the kitchen doorway.

Feeling sick with disgust, I walked towards the house. As I reached Mrs Hardwick, she lashed out with a slap that sent me reeling. My neck felt as though it had been dislocated.

"Get inside, you brazen little hussy," she hissed. She shoved me in the small of my back, propelling me into the hall. Then she pulled me round to face her and grasped my shoulders with iron-hard fingers.

"I have just about had it with you, young lady," she said. "If it weren't for the fact that there's an important guest staying tonight and we need every hand we've got, you'd be out of this house within five minutes."

I wanted to cry out at the unfairness of it but I knew that would be useless. Worse than useless. Any protest might get me thrown out right now, important guest or no important guest. And I had to keep my job, at least until Sophia and Robbie had escaped.

"Yes, Mrs Hardwick," I said meekly. "I'm very sorry, Mrs Hardwick."

She shoved me into the kitchen, where Polly was filling a hot water can.

"There's the best guest bedroom and dressing room to prepare, so you're going to have to work faster than you've ever worked in your life, young lady. They both want fires to take the chill off them, as well as linen and a thorough polish. You two will work together, and, Polly, don't let her out of your sight, or it'll be the high road for you too. She's not to be trusted for a second, you understand?"

"Yes, missus," said Polly.

"Er, missus, I need to empty this," I said, indicating the chamber pot.

Mrs Hardwick gave an incredulous snort. "You, madam, are not setting foot out of the house again tonight. See that she doesn't, Polly, or you know what will happen. Leave the chamber pot here. Nell will do it."

"Yes, missus," I said, relieved at not having to go anywhere near Jacob again.

As we scurried up to the bedrooms with our cleaning boxes, Polly whispered, "What have you done to put her in such a temper?"

The recollection of it made me feel sick again. "Jacob kissed me," I said, "and Mrs Hardwick saw."

Polly gave a little scream of delighted horror. "Oh, my, I can't believe you're still here. You sly little madam." She looked at me curiously. "Did you like it?"

"No! It was disgusting. He just grabbed me. And he stinks."

"You're lucky they need you today," she said, "or you'd have been out on your ear. Again."

"And what about him?"

"What do you mean?"

"Would he be out on his ear too?"

"Of course not."

"Why? He forced me. How come I'm the one in trouble and he gets away with it?"

Polly shrugged. "Because he's a man. Different rules."

"But that's so unfair. Don't you think it's unfair?"

"I suppose so. I've never really thought about it. It's just how things are."

"Well, it shouldn't be."

"Don't worry about Jacob. He'll get his comeuppance one day." She winked at me. "At least, he will if I have anything to do with it. You should have emptied that chamber pot over his head."

"I *should* have emptied it over his head. Why didn't I think of that?"

We had reached the guest bedroom, where Polly began a series of instructions. I tried to concentrate but I had greater worries on my mind.

If Jacob really had overheard my conversation with Robbie, and if he really was planning to tell Sir Henry, then Robbie and Sophia were in terrible danger. They would have to leave immediately if they were going to have any chance of getting away safely.

But Sophia was with her aunt in the White Parlour, no doubt being instructed in exactly how to accept Mr Ellerdale's proposal. And now that Polly had been charged with keeping me indoors, I couldn't take a message to Robbie without risking her job as well as my own.

I wrestled with the problem as I wrestled with the bed linen but I couldn't think of any way to warn them. And if I couldn't warn them in time, then Jacob might tell Sir Henry what Sophia was planning, and she really would be locked up for the rest of her life. And I would be stuck in the past forever.

CHAPTER TWENTY-SIX

Jacob
Speaks

For the next three hours I was kept constantly busy, making fires, fetching linen, carrying water and cleaning rooms, and I was never out of Polly's sight for a second. All that time, I racked my brains for a way to give a message to Sophia in secret. But she was never alone either. Once her aunt had finished with her, she was closeted in her dressing room with Madame Perrault, preparing for her engagement dinner.

Could I secretly slip her a note at the dinner table?

When Mrs Hardwick came to inspect the guest dressing room, I decided to give it a try.

"Would it help you, missus," I asked in what I hoped was a charming voice, "if I waited at table tonight? I think it would be good for me to get the experience."

Polly roared with laughter. The housekeeper gave me a withering look and left the room.

"Maidservants don't wait at table, Evie," said Polly when she had stopped laughing. "Not in houses like these. The family wouldn't want people to think they was poor."

"Why would people think they were poor?"

"We're cheap, aren't we? Lower wages, no livery and no tax to pay. If you can afford menservants, it shows you've got money to spare."

"So the men get higher wages?"

"Of course they do."

"What, because they work harder?" I said sarcastically.

Polly gave a scornful laugh. "Do they heck! But what do you expect when you employ a person just because they're tall and look good in livery?"

"What do you mean?"

"George got the job because he was six foot tall, the same height as the one what left. All the footmen in this house have to be six foot tall, so they fit the livery."

"Are you serious?"

"Would I lie to you? So no, you won't get to wait at table, unless you can turn yourself into a six-foot man."

So that was it. There was nothing to do but hope against hope that either Jacob was bluffing or that, if he did know something, he wouldn't take his knowledge to Sir Henry.

After all, if it was so hard for me, working in the house, to get a message to Sophia, how would a stable boy get to speak to the head of the household? Would he even dare try? Surely not. And if he did, Sir Henry probably wouldn't believe him. Imagine the stable boy telling Sir Henry Fane that his daughter was about to elope with the gardener! He'd probably be flogged for daring to suggest it.

No, Jacob's threat was just a trick to frighten me and then take advantage of my fear and confusion. I shuddered and wiped my mouth at the memory.

We had just sat down for supper when a man's raised voice stopped every conversation at the table. It seemed to be coming from the ground-floor entrance hall, right above us.

"What the devil do you mean by this?"

My heart thudded in my chest. It was Sir Henry.

The volume dropped to mumblings and murmurings. Sir Henry was talking to another man. Was it Jacob? Surely he wouldn't have gone to the front door. If there was one thing I knew by now about being a servant, it was that you never, ever used the front door.

The men stopped talking. The front door slammed. My heart was thumping. What should I do? What *could* I do?

George looked intrigued. "Who'd be at the door at this time of night?"

He got up and walked out. I itched to follow him but Mrs Hardwick was sitting at the head of the table, giving us all the evil eye.

After a couple of minutes, George returned.

"Well?" asked Betty as he sat down.

George shook his head and took a big bite of his bread. "Very odd," he said.

"What's odd?"

George took a swig of his beer.

"You saw nothing, did you?" said Mary.

"As a matter of fact, I did see something."

"Well, tell us then. I don't believe you saw anything at all."

"If you want to know, I saw the master himself, running across the stable yard towards the orchard."

"Evie, where do you think you're going?" shouted Mrs Hardwick. "Come back!"

But I was already out of the door. I had no idea how I was going to do it, but I had to stop Sir Henry discovering Robbie and Sophia.

In the stable yard, Jacob stepped out of the shadows, holding the overnight bag that Sophia had discarded in the wood the previous evening. "Look what I found," he said. "The master was very interested indeed in what I had to show him."

I swore at him as I raced past.

The orchard door stood wide open. I darted through. It was shadowy in the moonlight and I banged my head against a branch. I clutched it, moaning, and kept going, ducking through the trees. Illuminated in the moonlight at the far end, I saw two figures.

Sophia and Robbie.

Where was Sir Henry? Had he seen them yet? Was he watching them secretly?

"Sir Henry!" I called. "Come back! The house is on fire!"

If he was there, he didn't reveal himself. But Robbie and Sophia froze. Then they bolted, hand in hand, towards the gate that led to the Great Meadow.

A roar of fury filled the orchard. Sir Henry appeared from the shadows, crashing through the trees towards them. I raced towards him, thinking maybe I could trip him up. But he was too fast for me. He reached Robbie and Sophia and stood between them and the gate.

"You little hussy!" he bellowed, swiping Sophia across the face.

She cried out, staggered back and fell against a tree trunk. As she tried to right herself, he raised his hand again.

"Don't hit her!" Robbie shouted, grabbing his arm. "Don't you dare lay a finger on her, you bullying, evil—"

Sir Henry wheeled round, wrenched his arm free and punched Robbie in the jaw. Robbie reeled back.

"No!" screamed Sophia, but Sir Henry punched Robbie again and he stumbled and fell. Sir Henry swung his leg back to kick him.

"Leave him alone!" cried Sophia, running at her father like a battering ram. Unbalanced with his right foot in the air, he fell heavily on his left side, hitting his head against a tree root.

"Sit on him!" I shouted, plonking myself down on his stomach. He roared in fury and raised his hand to slap me, but Sophia hurled herself on to his chest. His breath stank of alcohol.

"Evie?" Sophia said, staring in wonder.

"Pin his arms down!"

We grabbed an arm each, but Sir Henry was too strong for us. He wrenched his arms away and gave

Sophia a terrific slap on the other side of her face. "You filthy, disgusting—"

Robbie scrambled to his feet, pulled Sophia up and stepped in front of her. "How dare you hit your daughter, you coward? Here, hit me instead."

Sir Henry threw me off his stomach as though I was a rag doll. I fell back into a bush. He got to his feet and squared up to Robbie. Robbie threw a punch and Sir Henry punched back. They were going to kill each other and I had no idea what to do.

Suddenly, from out of the shadows, appeared Mr Paxton, the butler. He stepped neatly between Robbie and Sir Henry. "Sir," he said, "allow me to deal with this young miscreant, if you will."

Sir Henry actually seemed to listen to Mr Paxton. He took a step back.

The butler turned to Robbie and pointed to the gate. "Leave the premises this instant. Never set foot on Sir Henry's land again."

Sir Henry trembled with rage. "If he sets foot on my land again, I'll shoot him myself."

Robbie looked at Sophia. "I cannot leave you here like this," he said. "Come with me."

"Come with you?" roared Sir Henry. "Why, you scoundrel, you—" He lunged for Robbie, but Mr Paxton held him back.

"Go," Sophia begged Robbie. "Go, or you will make things worse."

Robbie looked at her in agony.

"Bring me my pistol!" Sir Henry yelled to the butler, struggling to get out of his grasp.

Robbie looked Sir Henry in the eye. "I am leaving, sir." He walked out of the orchard gate and disappeared into the darkness of the Great Meadow.

Sir Henry turned to Sophia. He looked as though he was itching to strike her again. "As for you, you lying, cheating little snake... Telling me you had seen the error of your ways, accepting Ellerdale's proposal, when all the time you were planning to sneak out of the house and give yourself to a filthy little gardener. Fetch me my whip!" he roared at the butler.

"Sir Henry," said Mr Paxton, "I wonder if it might be better for Miss Fane to return to the house quietly."

"After what she has done? Never!"

"I understand your anger, of course, sir, but you have a guest, and it might be prudent for Miss Fane to return to her room, for the time being."

"She has no room in my house," said Sir Henry. "She can starve in the streets for all I care. I want nothing to do with her ever again."

Sophia was trembling, but she met her father's eye with a defiant glare.

"Sir Henry," said the butler, "I would suggest that we would wish to avoid gossip and scandal in the neighbourhood. It might not be quite wise to have Miss Fane thrown into the streets. Perhaps if she were to be confined to her room..."

Sir Henry rounded on his daughter. "To think of all I have lavished on you. And for what, you ungrateful, deceitful, sly little brat?" He spat on the ground in front of her and then he turned to Mr Paxton. "Take her to her room. Fix bolts to the door and bars to the window. From this day forward, I have no daughter."

CHAPTER TWENTY-SEVEN

A Promise

Sir Henry strode away through the trees. The butler took Sophia's arm. She made no attempt to resist. Head down, she walked silently back to the house.

I crouched under the bush, my heart hammering.

What an idiot I was, to imagine I could change the past. As if anybody in the world had ever been able to change the past.

What would happen to me now?

It was too terrifying to think about. I felt as though I was trapped in a never-ending tunnel.

Everything was ruined. Now Sophia would be locked up for the rest of her life. And Robbie...

Where would Robbie go?

Suddenly I came to life. I ran out of the orchard gate and down through the Great Meadow, stumbling over the rough grass. If he was walking, I should be able to catch him up.

"Evie?"

I stopped, my eyes straining through the gloom.

"Evie, it's me. Robbie."

I could see him walking towards me now. "Oh, Robbie, thank goodness."

"What are you doing? Did he throw you out too?"

"No, I came to find you."

"I was under that elm tree by the wall," he said. "I could go no further. It took all my strength not to go back in there. I must get her out. I cannot lurk outside the walls and save my own skin while she is being tortured inside the house."

"She's not being tortured," I said, hoping I was right.

"I will come tomorrow and fetch her," he said. "I cannot leave her here."

"You can't come back. You heard what he said. He'll shoot you. You were lucky he didn't kill you then. He would have done, if Mr Paxton hadn't turned up. And how would it help Sophia if you were dead?"

"What good am I doing her now," he said wildly, "standing uselessly aside while she is locked up and beaten?"

Suddenly I felt older than Robbie. He was far too much in love to think straight. I was going to have to sort this out myself.

A new courage began to grow inside me. Mum had always gone on about how stubborn I was. Well, now, I thought, I'm going to put my stubbornness to good use for once.

"Sir Henry is a bully," I said to Robbie, "and you can't let bullies win. You have to show them you're stronger than them."

Robbie looked at me doubtfully.

"Not by brute force," I said. "He's always going

228

to win that way. We're going to have to use cunning instead. I mean, I work in the house all day, don't I? I sleep in the house. We know exactly where Sophia will be the whole time. How hard can it be to get her out?"

"Her father will keep her under lock and key. He will keep the door guarded."

"Don't worry," I said. "I'm in the house the whole time. I'll find a way."

Then my stomach plummeted.

I wasn't in the house now, was I? I had bolted in the middle of supper. I was going to be sacked, and then how would Sophia escape?

"I need to get back," I said, trying to keep my voice calm. "Just tell me where you'll be and how I can send messages to you."

He looked blank for a minute. Then he said, "I shall go to my mother's friend, Elizabeth. She lives in the white cottage next to the church. I shall make sure nobody sees me arrive, and I shall stay hidden during the day."

"But how will I get a message to you?"

"Betty lives in the village," he said. "Send news by Betty. Write nothing down, mind."

A picture came into my head of Betty in a gossipy huddle with Mary and Alice. "Can she keep a secret?"

"I have known her all my life. I'm sure we can trust her."

I opened my mouth to voice my doubts but then I closed it again. What choice did we have?

"Leave it to me," I said, sounding a lot more confident than I felt. "I'll get Sophia out."

"Thank you, Evie. Thank you so much."

I hitched up my skirt and ran. Outside the scullery door I paused to catch my breath and collect my thoughts. What was I going to tell Mrs Hardwick? What excuse could I possibly make? Why would anybody run outside in the middle of a meal like that?

And then it came to me. Maybe, if I really grovelled, it might just work.

CHAPTER TWENTY-EIGHT

An Idea

"Vomiting?" said Mrs Hardwick. She didn't sound at all convinced.

I nodded, screwing up my nose in disgust. "Really bad. It came on all of a sudden. I didn't have time to tell you. I must have eaten too much beef at dinner. And I thought – for everybody's sakes – that I ought to get as far away from the house as possible."

Mrs Hardwick's eyes were still narrowed, but she took a step back, which seemed like a good sign.

"And it's over?"

"I think so. And I didn't want to miss any more work. I'm so sorry, especially since you've been so busy tonight."

"Hmm." She still sounded sceptical.

"I know I haven't been the best housemaid so far," I said in my humblest voice, "but I'm learning, and I really want to make a success of it. I'll miss my breaks for as long as you like, and I promise I'll work twice as hard from now on."

"You'll need to," she said, "if you want to be half as good as Polly."

"I know," I said, surprised and pleased. "Polly is amazing."

It took me ages to get to sleep, and then my sleep was filled with horrible nightmares. Robbie and Sophia and Sir Henry and Mrs Hardwick and Jacob swirled through my dreams in increasingly terrifying scenarios. The worst one – the one that jolted me awake with a pounding heart at three in the morning – was the one in which I was dragged off to be hanged for sitting on Sir Henry Fane.

I felt no better when I woke up. I probably would be hanged for that. Polly had told me an awful story yesterday about a twelve-year-old girl in the next town who was hanged for stealing a petticoat.

Mrs Hardwick, carrying a breakfast tray into the servants' hall, frowned at me. "You do look peaky."

I was surprised and touched. I couldn't believe Mrs Hardwick was actually concerned about my well-being.

"I hope you're not infectious," she said. "I don't want you spreading anything to the rest of the staff."

Oh. Of course.

"Miss Fane still locked in then?" asked George, looking at the tray.

"She is," said Mrs Hardwick in a tone that dared anybody to ask another question. "Take this to her room, Polly. And remember to lock the door when you come out."

"I'll do it," I said.

Outside Sophia's room, I set down the tray. Two

new bolts had been fixed to the door.

When I walked in, Sophia was sitting in a little chair drawn up to the window, scratching at the bottom pane with something she held in her right hand.

"Miss Fane?"

Sophia continued to scratch the glass. She was dressed in the same clothes she had been wearing last night. Her hair had come loose and sections of it tumbled down her back.

I put the tray on the bedside table and walked towards her.

There were three words etched on the window.

Sophia Fane
Imprisoned

Sophia's cheeks were white and there were purple shadows under her red-rimmed eyes. She looked blank and hollowed out.

"Did you sleep at all?" I asked.

She shook her head.

"Were you writing on the glass all night?"

"If I am to spend the rest of my life in this room, I want the people who live here after me to know that I was kept a prisoner by my own father. I want my name to be remembered, at least."

"Has your father said you'll spend the rest of your life here?"

"He has made that very clear. And better that than that I should betray my heart and marry a man

I despise, in order that Charles Ellerdale should increase his estate and my father should get his hands on Ellerdale's money. They can marry each other if they want to. I shall die here, alone."

"But what about Robbie? You can't just give up on all your plans."

Sophia jumped to her feet, her dark eyes flashing. "Give up?" she said in a fierce whisper. "You speak as though I have a choice. Do you not think I would have bolted from the room the moment you opened the door, if it would not have put Robbie in mortal danger?"

"Well, I—"

"If I attempt to run away, my father will have Robbie hunted down and killed."

"I'm sorry. I shouldn't have said that. I know you wouldn't give up on him."

Sophia looked at me and her stiffness softened slightly. "You came to the orchard last night. You tried to help. Thank you."

"Robbie is waiting for you," I whispered. "He's staying with a friend in the village, waiting for a message. As soon as you can come to him, he will be ready, and you can run away."

Sophia's eyes, which had lit up with hope when I started to speak, now darkened again. "How can I go to him without being caught? Even if I could leave this room, how could I leave the house? Everywhere is locked at night, and in the daytime I could never leave unseen. It is impossible."

"Nothing's impossible. We just haven't come up

with the right idea yet."

Sophia looked at me curiously. "Why are you so concerned for us, Evie?"

It was a good question. It was just a shame that I couldn't tell her the answer: that I was clinging on to the desperate hope that I had come into the past for a reason, and that once I had kept my promise to help Sophia, I would be able to return to my own time.

And also, I knew what would happen if she didn't escape. I knew that she was already pregnant and that, if she didn't get out of here, her baby would be taken away from her as soon as it was born. I knew that her spirit was still not at peace, two hundred years after she was imprisoned. If I could help to reunite her with Robbie, then perhaps her ghost would finally be laid to rest.

Sophia was looking at me, waiting for an answer.

"It's complicated," I said.

"You are a very unusual servant, Evie," she said. "How old are you?"

"Thirteen."

"You look older. I thought you were my age."

We did look about the same age. It was partly that I looked older than thirteen, and partly that Sophia looked younger than sixteen. This morning she looked even younger than usual, with her hair tumbling down her back. It was the same length as my hair, I realised. And exactly the same colour.

We were the same height too. And the same build. Even our eyes were the same colour.

My eyes opened very wide.

What if...?

Might it be possible?

But when could we do it?

It would have to be before the house was locked up for the night. But not in daylight.

Dusk, then.

A terrifying thought twisted my stomach into knots. Would I still be here at dusk?

"Miss Fane," I asked, "did your father mention me last night?"

Sophia frowned. "You?"

"Did he say he was going to sack me?"

"Sack you?"

"For sitting on him. Is he going to sack me for it?"

"I have no idea what you are talking about," she said. "What does this mean, to 'sack' you?"

I almost growled in frustration. Yet another word that clearly wasn't used that way in 1814.

"Throw me out then," I said. "Will he throw me out of the house?"

"I cannot imagine," she said, "that he has any recollection of you whatsoever."

Oh, please let that be true, I prayed. If I didn't get sacked today, then my idea might just work. It was our best chance anyway.

I mustn't arouse suspicion by staying too long in her room. I would have to be quick.

"Miss Fane," I said, "I might have thought of a way to get you out. A way that will mean you won't be seen leaving. Can I tell you my idea?"

CHAPTER TWENTY-NINE

The
Escape

At seven o'clock, carrying an empty chamber pot, I entered Sophia's room.

She was sitting at the window, staring at the darkening garden. She whipped her head round as I walked in. Her hair was wild and tangled, as though she had spent hours running her fingers through it. She jumped up from her chair.

"Oh, Evie, you're here! I was so frightened that something would prevent you from coming."

I looked at the pane of glass in the bottom left-hand corner of the window. It now said:

Sophia Fane
Imprisoned here
27th April 1814

"We don't have much time," I said. "Mrs Hardwick has been watching me like a hawk all day. Betty's just left. She's going to tell Robbie to wait for you at the stile by the three elm trees in Church Meadow."

Sophia's eyes lit up with excitement. "We shall walk overnight to Lower Mistleham, and from there we shall take the stagecoach to London. I have money in my pocket and Robbie has saved enough from his wages for the journey to Scotland and back. And when we return and set up home in London…" She lowered her voice. "I will sell my jewels."

"Your diamond ring?" I asked.

"That, yes. But also—" She glanced across the room. "Guard the door."

I stood with my back against it. Sophia opened the bottom drawer of her desk and from under some sheets of paper pulled out a small hammer and a flat-ended metal tool.

She walked to the bed and dropped to her knees on the carpet. She pushed the bed towards the wall. It was on castors and rolled back easily.

She folded back the corner of the carpet. Then she took the metal tool and edged it under a nail in one of the floorboards. The board was shorter than the rest and the nails at each corner were very slightly raised.

I watched as she levered up all four nails. Then she eased her fingertips into the gaps at either end and lifted the board away.

Sitting snugly in the void between the joists was a wooden box, about the size of a large shoebox. Sophia set it on the floor, lifted the hinged lid and took out a bracelet: a row of blood-red rubies between two rows of glittering diamonds. She draped it over her wrist.

"Wow," I said. "That's so beautiful."

Sophia smiled. "My grandmother gave it to me.

Not my father's mother. She was horrible. But my maternal grandmother was lovely. She left all her jewels to my mother, but when I was thirteen and she was dying, she summoned me to her bedside and gave me this bracelet. She told me not to tell a soul. 'If you ever need money,' she said, 'sell this.'"

"It's amazing."

"I should have had my mother's jewels too, of course, but they were put away until I was of age." She gave a sad little laugh. "Now I shall never see them again."

Footsteps sounded outside. Sophia, still on her knees, pushed the bracelet under the folds of her dress and flipped the carpet back over the floorboards. I moved the bed into place and busied myself with smoothing the covers.

The footsteps faded away down the corridor. Sophia slipped the bracelet into her pocket, pushed the bed aside and replaced the empty box between the joists. She repositioned the floorboard and hammered the nails in.

"Right," I said, moving the bed into place again. "We need to work fast."

"Unhook my buttons," said Sophia. "Then I'll do yours."

She talked to me in an excited whisper as I fumbled with the tiny satin-covered buttons down the back of her dress. "We shall change our names, of course, as soon as we are married. We shall sell the bracelet and rent a little house in London. And we shall use the rest of the money to campaign to end child labour and ensure that every child can go to school and learn to read and write."

"But how will you do that?" I asked.

"Oh, we have many ideas. And we shall dedicate our whole lives to the campaign." She was practically fizzing with excitement now. "When Robbie and I are together, there will be no end to the things we can accomplish."

I undid the final button. "Here, you do mine now."

"I have never unbuttoned a dress," said Sophia, "except on my dolls."

I gaped at her in disbelief. Then I tried to rearrange my expression as though I thought it was normal for a sixteen-year-old girl never to have dressed or undressed herself.

Sophia's excitement had disappeared. She looked completely flat. "I suppose I should learn," she said in a small voice. "Things will be different now." She moved to the back of my dress and started unbuttoning it.

I was suddenly filled with fear that she was about to change her mind.

"How long will it take you to reach Gretna Green?" I asked, hoping to bring back her excitement.

"At least two days, I think, from London."

"So I shall have to stay here for two days," I said.

She frowned in thought. "You will have to remain much longer than that. Once we are married, it will take at least two days to return to London. And we shan't be safe while we are travelling. My father will be sure to send messages to all the coaching inns along the way. It will be at least a week until we are safely in lodgings under a different name."

A *week*? How would I stand being locked in this room, alone, for a whole week, worrying all the time that I might be found out?

Then I realised what I was thinking and almost slapped myself for my stupidity. Because it wasn't up to me, was it? I couldn't decide how long I stayed in the past. If I could, the situation would be a lot less stressful.

"A week is fine," I said. "It will be a nice rest, sitting in a room all day. Better than emptying slops and scrubbing floors."

"There," said Sophia, stepping away from me. "All done. Now let us change clothes."

Ten minutes later we stood facing each other. I couldn't believe how luxurious Sophia's silk gown felt after the coarse, itchy fabric of my maid's outfit.

She sat at her dressing table in my plain, ill-fitting dress and apron. "Now, Evie, take the pins out of my hair and brush it."

I raised my eyebrows. "Brush your own hair!"

Sophia looked shocked. "But my maid does my hair."

"Well, you don't have a maid any more, remember? You *are* a maid now, so you'd better get used to it." I pulled over a chair and sat next to her. "Shove up. I need to look in the mirror too."

Wordlessly, Sophia shoved up. I undid my bun and took one of the ebony-backed hairbrushes off the dressing table. Sophia slowly reached her hands to her head and began to pull the scattered pins out of her hair.

We brushed our hair in silence, falling into unison on the strokes.

Sophia glanced at my reflection and her eyes widened.

"Gracious, Evie, you look exactly like me!"

I looked at our reflections. At the two pairs of brown eyes set in two heart-shaped faces, framed by dark hair with a touch of copper.

"It's extraordinary," she said. "We could be sisters."

"Yes. We really could."

Sophia frowned.

"What?" I asked.

"Your hair."

She ran her hands through my hair in all directions, ruffling it violently.

"Get off! Ow, you're pulling! What are you doing?"

"That's better," she said, disentangling her hands. "It was far too neat. You ought not to have brushed it."

"Would you like me to do your hair like mine and Polly's?"

"Do," she said. "I shall watch you carefully, since I shall have to do it myself in future."

She sat in a tense silence while I scraped her hair back and twisted it into a bun. Suddenly she said, "I'm frightened."

"Of your father catching you?"

"No, no. If you are here in my room, being me, he will not even know I am gone. That is the beauty of your idea."

"So what are you frightened of?"

"I know nothing, Evie. In my entire life, I have never even done my own hair. I cannot cook, I cannot clean, I cannot make a fire…"

"You'll learn," I said. "Robbie will teach you. I didn't know any of those things either, until I started work here. There," I said, sticking the last pin in her bun. "Look at you now. Evie the housemaid."

Sophia reached round and took my hand. "Sit next to me."

We sat together at the dressing table in silence, gazing at our reflections. I looked at my wild, tangled hair and thought of the girl at the window in the white nightdress.

"You have done so much for me," Sophia said. "I wish there were something I could do for you."

"Don't worry about that," I said. "I'll be fine. But if there was something you could do for Polly, maybe? I was teaching her to read and write. She really wants to learn."

And as I said the words, I remembered what Robbie had said about how he had taught himself.

"When you were learning to read and write," I asked, "did you use a primer?"

"I did," she said. "Would you like Polly to have it?"

"That would be great. Then she could carry on

learning. She wants to be a housekeeper some day, you see."

"All my school books are in there," said Sophia, pointing to a big carved cupboard on the other side of the room. "Take anything you wish for Polly."

"Thank you," I said. "I'll find a way to get them to her. You must go, or Mrs Hardwick will be on your case. And believe me, you don't want that."

Sophia reached into her pocket and pressed two gold coins into my hand. "Here. You may need these."

"Oh, no," I said, handing them back. "It's really kind, but you'll need them for your journey."

She curled my fingers around the coins. "I have sufficient. You must take these. For emergencies."

I remembered my mother's words at Victoria Station. In another time, another world.

"Thank you," I said. "That's really kind of you." I stood up and slipped the coins into my pocket.

"What must I do when I go down?" asked Sophia.

"Take this chamber pot with you. Don't worry," I said, as she recoiled. "It's empty. But you'll need it. It's the only reason for a housemaid to go outside. Leave by the back door in the basement. Hopefully everyone will be busy and won't see you leave. Keep your head down as you cross the stable yard, and if that horrible Jacob tries to grab you, smack him in the face from me."

I decided not to mention I'd been banned from leaving the house. At this time of day, Mrs Hardwick was always in her room, doing the accounts, so I was pretty sure Sophia would be able to leave without being questioned.

"If you're holding this," I said, "anyone who sees you will think you're going to empty it on the compost heap. So walk in that direction and hide it in the woods once you're out of sight. Then get away as fast as you can."

Sophia was scrutinising me. "If you keep your hair around your face," she said, "and do not look directly at the servants – no, better still, stay face down on the bed when a servant is in the room – yes, if you make sure you do not show your face to anybody, then I think all will be well."

"It will be fine," I said. "Now you really must go. Good luck. With everything."

She gave me a quick, fierce hug. "Thank you, Evie. You have been so very good to me. I shall remember you always."

"Make sure you bolt the door behind you," I said. "And don't forget this." I held out the chamber pot and smiled. "It's your passport to the outside world."

CHAPTER THIRTY

A Discovery

Birds were singing outside the window.

It felt late. Why hadn't Polly woken me?

I opened my eyes a fraction and peered out blurrily. My stomach churned.

I was in Sophia's room, in Sophia's clothes, in Sophia's bed.

Why hadn't I gone back to the present? Had Sophia been caught?

But she couldn't have been. Because if she had been caught, then I would have been caught too.

I went cold all over. Why had I never thought of this before? If Sophia was caught, then I would be found out as an impersonator, and I would be hanged without a shadow of a doubt. That was if Sir Henry didn't shoot me or whip me to death first.

I burrowed down into the bedclothes, my head in my hands. My throat tightened and I couldn't breathe.

I hadn't gone back to the present. I hadn't made anything better. Things were as bad as they could possibly be. Not only was I stuck in the past, but now I had become Sophia Fane. And I would either be found out and killed, or I would be locked in this room for the rest of my life.

Footsteps sounded along the corridor. Sophia's dressing-room door opened. I forced myself to breathe, fighting the tightness in my throat and chest.

"I always thought there was something strange about her," said a voice. "Something a bit odd."

"Well, I liked her," said Polly. "She was a terrible scatterbrain, but she was kind and she made me laugh. I shall miss her."

"She took her box, did she?"

It was Mary's voice. Had Mary replaced me already?

"She had no box," said Polly. "She came with nothing but the clothes she stood up in."

"You see," said Mary, "it's very odd. Everyone but the poorest scrap of a workhouse girl has a box. And she didn't look a bit like a pauper. Bursting with health, she looked."

"Her teeth were lovely," said Polly. "Whiter than pearls, they were."

"And yet she came with nothing and she left with nothing. It makes no sense. I'd have thought she'd have told you something, at least."

I felt terrible. I'd desperately wanted to leave Polly a letter. Even though she couldn't read yet, she could have asked George to read it aloud to her. I had sneaked a piece of paper from Sir Henry's desk while I was dusting his study yesterday, but then Mrs Hardwick came in before I could find a pencil. So I had left Polly without a word.

But at least I could write her a letter while I was locked up in here, and leave it for her to find.

"Maybe she'll come back," said Polly.

Mary snorted. "Can you imagine Hardwitch taking her back after she's run off like that? She was in enough trouble before."

"She'll have gone to her mother in London," Polly said. "Homesick, she was, I think, though she tried to hide it."

"Ah," said Mary. "So she bolted. Like that little thing we had last year – what was her name?"

"Sarah," said Polly. "Poor little scrap. Only eight, she was. I wonder what became of her."

"I need to be getting back to the laundry," said Mary, "or I'll never get done."

"Thanks for giving me a hand," said Polly. "It's no fun doing this alone. I hope Hardwitch finds somebody else soon."

"Well, with any luck she'll find somebody better than Evie."

"She was a shocking housemaid," said Polly as they left the room. "Couldn't even light a fire. But she was teaching me to read and write. I don't reckon the next one will be able to do that."

It was so weird to hear people talk about me as though I wasn't there. As though I was no longer in their lives.

And I was no longer in their lives, was I?

Or I was, but not as Evie.

Panic rose in me again. I pushed the heavy bedclothes off and made myself take deep, slow breaths. And a glimmer of hope flickered inside my head. Sophia had said it would be a week before they were back from Scotland and living in London under new names. So maybe I would just be stuck in the past for a week, until they were safe.

"The master's having bars put on the window tomorrow," said Mary. "Not that she'd have a hope of escaping through there. Not if she wanted to make it out alive."

A little voice wormed its way into my mind. *You're Sophia Fane now. And Sophia Fane was locked in here for the rest of her life.*

I pushed the thought away.

It was easier than I had expected to spend whole days lying face down on the bed, my hair spread over the pillows in a tangled mess, drifting in and out of sleep. I stayed face down whenever Polly or Mary came in with the food tray, cringing with embarrassment as they took away my chamber pot.

When Polly came in alone, I ached to confide in her. It was torture to have her so close and yet not to be able to speak. But if she knew, then she would be in terrible danger too. So I stayed face down on the bed and said nothing.

Sometimes I wondered who I was. Everyone here thought I was Sophia, of course. I knew I wasn't Sophia, but I didn't feel like myself either.

I wasn't Evie the housemaid any longer: that Evie had disappeared. But neither was I the twenty-first century Evie, who lived in London with her mother.

Did that Evie even exist any more? Had she ever existed? What if this was reality, and that life had all been a dream?

Was I going mad?

During the long afternoons, when no servant came near my room, I sat in the chair by the window, looking out over the gardens, just as Sophia had done when she was scratching those words on the glass.

The gardens were changing every day. New leaves unfurled on the trees; the grass deepened to a brighter shade of green; flowers blossomed in the sun. I opened the window, smelled the fresh air and felt the breeze on my face. Sometimes, when the wind was in the right direction, I even caught the scent of flowers. But it was nothing like actually walking through the gardens, feeling the grass under my feet, stroking the velvety apple blossom, seeing a robin so close that I could make out its individual feathers, watching the sun's rays light on a dewdrop and create a tiny rainbow in its glittering sphere.

Sleeping in snatches, spending tortured hours awake in the middle of the night and dozing through the mornings, time became muddled. What date was it? Had it been a week yet? I needed to start recording the days.

I went to Sophia's desk and took out a quill pen, a bottle of ink and a couple of sheets of writing paper. I would write to Polly too, and leave the letter under my pillow for her to find if I ever did go back to the present.

The door at the end of the corridor opened. Footsteps approached. I gathered up the writing things and dived under the bedcovers with them. I spread my hair over my face and tucked my work-ruined hands out of sight.

Voices. Polly, definitely. And it sounded like George and William.

The bolts slid back and the door opened.

"You don't really think they would have, do you?" said Polly in a hushed voice.

"Shh, Miss Fane's sleeping," said William.

"She's always sleeping," said George. "I reckon he's drugged her."

"Don't say things like that," said Polly.

George laughed. "You're a fine one to talk."

"I wasn't gossiping about the family. Now, which furniture are you meant to be taking?"

"All of it," said George. "And the pictures and ornaments. She's to be left with nothing but the bed, the master said."

"Poor thing," said Polly. "It really will be a prison. She's been locked up for eight days and it must already feel like a lifetime to her. How can he think of keeping her locked up for the rest of her life? She'll be driven mad."

Eight days since Sophia was locked up. I had swapped places with her the day after it happened, so I had been here exactly a week. If things had worked out, then Sophia and Robbie should be safely married and back in London by now. Did that mean I might be able to go back to the present tonight?

"Let's move the dressing table first," said William. "Clear all this stuff off the top, Polly."

I heard drawers being opened and things being moved around.

"But do you really think they would have done?" asked Polly in a lower voice. "Robbie and Evie?"

I stiffened.

"Well, it's all over the village," said George.

"But do you believe it?"

"It seems a bit of a coincidence, that's all I'm saying. Both of them disappearing on the same night. Slipped out of his aunt's cottage without a word, he did. Told his aunt he was going to bed. She only discovered he was gone when he didn't appear the next morning."

"And that was the same night Evie disappeared?"

"The very same."

Nobody spoke for a minute. I heard the sounds of ornaments being taken off the mantelpiece.

"He was a bit odd, that Robbie," said George. "Never seemed to quite fit in here."

"He was very gentle," said Polly. "I liked him. He was kind."

"That's what I mean. He was different. Never joined in any of the wrestling or sport. Always reading or drawing."

"Well, I hope they've both found something better than this," said Polly. They worked in silence for a while, and then she said, "It's strange how people come and go. I never even knew Evie's surname. Or Robbie's, come to that."

"Robbie told me his," said William. "I remembered it because it was unusual. Robbie Tregarron, he was."

The hairs stood up on the back of my neck.

"Tregarron?" said Polly. "What a funny name."

"That's what I said. He said it was Cornish."

Goose pimples prickled all over my body.

"Not that he'd ever lived in Cornwall," said William. "But his father came from a tiny Cornish hamlet. Then the place was infected with smallpox and his father's family all died. The hamlet was wiped out. Like a ghost village, it was. Robbie's father left and went to London. Walked the whole way. Took him weeks, sleeping in hedgerows and living on berries. But he found work in London and married there, and that's where Robbie was born."

"And then Robbie's whole family died too," said Polly.

"Yes," said William. "Robbie said he was the only Tregarron still alive."

"Better get this chest moved," said George. "You take that end, Will."

Polly's sleeve brushed mine as she reached under the bed for the chamber pot. And then they all left, and the bolts were drawn across the door again.

I pulled myself upright. My heart was beating so fast I could hardly breathe.

Only one family with that name. From a hamlet in Cornwall.

Robbie was my ancestor.

CHAPTER THIRTY-ONE

A Parting

I was filled with a crazy, restless energy. I swung my legs out of bed. I had to move.

Up and down the room I walked, repeating the names over and over in my head.

Robbie Tregarron. Evie Tregarron.

And then I had a thought that stopped me in my tracks.

If Robbie and Sophia had got married, then Sophia Fane was now Sophia Tregarron. So that was why Mum and I looked so like Sophia. She was our ancestor too. And so was their baby.

Was that why the ghost had only appeared to me and Mum? Because only somebody deeply connected with Sophia, and who looked so similar to her, could travel back in time and swap places with her so that she could escape?

Thirteen years ago, Mum had refused Sophia's summons. But I had accepted it. And it looked as though my purpose had actually been achieved at last. So might I be able to go home?

It was very late and my candle had burned down

to a tiny stump. George and William had been in and out of the room all afternoon, stripping it of Sophia's possessions, so it was evening before I was able to start my letter to Polly. It was partly to thank her for everything, and partly to encourage her to continue reading and writing so she could get to be a housekeeper one day.

As well as that letter, I wrote a note in an imitation of Sophia's handwriting, using the writing on the window as my guide. The note explained that Evie had given the letter to Sophia for safekeeping, to pass on to Polly when the time was right.

I blew on the paper to dry the ink, and then I took Sophia's two gold coins from my pocket, placed them in the middle of the paper and folded the sheets around the money. On the outside I wrote Polly's name, and then I slipped the letter with the money inside it under my pillow, along with the schoolbooks I had taken from Sophia's cupboard.

The stable clock struck midnight. And it seemed as if the world was suddenly covered with a blanket of silence.

Tap, tap, tap.

My heart stopped.

The tapping sounded again.

Dizzy with anticipation, I got out of bed, walked to the window and drew back the curtains.

And there was Sophia outside the window, in her white nightdress. She didn't look wild and desperate any more. The expression on her face was calm and serene.

She placed her left hand on the window, exactly as she had done before. I placed my right hand against the glass to meet it. And then I saw, on her fourth finger, a slim gold wedding ring.

Her eyes met mine and she smiled. As I smiled back, she began to fade away, her features melting into the moonlit night.

"No," I whispered. "Don't go."

But a cloud passed across the moon and Sophia dissolved into the darkness.

I stood at the window, staring into the night, willing her to come back. But I knew she wouldn't. She was married to Robbie now, and she would be able to keep her baby.

All of a sudden a fog came over my brain. My limbs felt heavy and I could barely keep my eyes open long enough to stumble into bed and lay my head on the pillow. As I sank into the mattress, I thought I heard the high metallic strike of Anna's living-room clock, chiming the strokes of midnight.

PART THREE

*To every thing there is a season, and a time to every purpose
under the heaven:*
*A time to be born, and a time to die; a time to plant, and a
time to pluck up that which is planted;*
*A time to kill, and a time to heal; a time to break down, and a
time to build up;*
*A time to weep, and a time to laugh; a time to mourn, and a
time to dance;*
*A time to cast away stones, and a time to gather stones
together; a time to embrace, and a time to refrain from
embracing;*
*A time to get, and a time to lose; a time to keep, and a time to
cast away;*
*A time to rend, and a time to sew; a time to keep silence, and
a time to speak;*
*A time to love, and a time to hate; a time of war, and a time
of peace.*

Ecclesiastes, Chapter 3, Verses 1–8

CHAPTER THIRTY-TWO

A Time
to Mourn

Swish, clatter, swish, clatter, swish.

Strange. Somebody was washing dishes really close to my room.

My bed felt different. The room smelled different.

I opened my eyes and my heart missed a beat. My suitcase lay open on the floor, my clothes strewn around it. The sound of a radio mingled with the washing-up noises. Outside, a car swooshed past.

I shrieked with delight. I was back! Really back! Back in the twenty-first century!

Joy and relief washed over me in waves. It had worked! I had done what I needed to do, and I was back in my own life again. Back in the world of running water and wifi and friends and TV and flushing toilets and central heating and chocolate and crisps and phones and Mum. Real life.

My life.

I whirled around the room with sheer happiness until I got so dizzy that I crashed into the wall. I was about to run into the living room (I was so happy that I could even have hugged Anna) when I caught a whiff of my own smell, and realised I was not in a fit state to encounter another human being. Not in the twenty-first century anyway.

I stood in the shower and stared at the water pouring down on me. What an incredible invention. Hot running water, as much as you needed, right there, in the pipes, waiting for you to turn on the tap. No fires, no coppers, no cans to be carried up and down stairs, no slops to be taken out to the garden. Just clean hot water, whenever you needed it. And the dirty water washed away, out of sight, without anyone having to lift a finger. In every house in the country.

Why didn't people talk more about this miracle?

It felt amazing to be clean again, and to smell of shower gel and shampoo instead of vinegar and soot. I put on a pair of jeans and a jumper and headed for the kitchen.

Anna had cleared a space around the skull at the dining table. A notebook lay open in front of her, the page covered in scrawly handwriting. She was leafing through a pile of large black-and-white photos. She glanced up as I walked in.

"Good morning."

"Morning," I said, trying to speak in a normal voice while my mind attempted to process this incredible fact. From the perfectly ordinary way she had greeted me, it was obvious that the whole time I had spent in the past had taken no time at all in the present.

Anna looked at me more closely and frowned.

"You look exhausted. Did you have a bad night?"

I considered the question.

"Not entirely bad," I said, "but not exactly restful either."

"I've got to shoot off, I'm afraid," she said, grabbing her bag from the table. "Site meetings at the burial ground. Do you want to come along?"

"Oh, er, no, I'll stay here, thanks. Homework and stuff, you know." I walked over to my food cupboard to find something for breakfast.

"Do you want the heating on?" asked Anna. "It's that switch by the door."

I flicked the switch down.

"Chilly this morning, isn't it?" she said. "But the flat warms up in no time once the heating's on."

I thought of the hours it had taken every day to keep a room warm in 1814: cleaning out ashes, laying fires, lugging coal buckets, trying to coax sparks from flint and steel. And now we could heat an entire house at the flick of a switch. Never again would I take that magic for granted.

When Anna left, I felt restless. I took the spare set of keys and headed outside.

The garden hit me like a slap in the face. Instead of flowerbeds and lawns and hedges alive with blossom and birdsong, I was faced with the grey tarmac car park and the strip of grass bordered by bare wooden fence panels. The background noise was the dull drone of car engines from the main road in the distance.

I walked round to the side of the house. Anna had said the stable clock was still there, so maybe the

261

developers had left the stable block alone.

At the entrance to the yard was a gate with a smart sign on it: **The Old Stables**. The stables and the laundry building had been converted into houses. There were paving stones where the cobbles used to be, and all the doors and windows were modern. But the bricks looked the same, just a little more weather-beaten, and so did the tiled roof with the clock tower on the top. The clock's golden hands stood at exactly twelve o'clock. I glanced at my watch. It was half past ten.

The gate was locked. I turned back and walked past the front of the house again, round to the left, where the lawns and flower gardens had once stretched all the way to the fields. Now there was only a narrow path bordered by a high fence.

I walked to the back of the house, where the arched doors in the old brick wall used to lead to the kitchen garden and the orchard. The wall had gone, and so had the orchard and the garden. There was just a tiny fenced-in patio with a plastic table and chairs. And beyond the patio, more houses.

Surely they'd have left the wood though. They couldn't have cut down the bluebell wood. They wouldn't have been allowed to.

But there was no wood. There was nothing to suggest that there had ever been a wood. There was just a bare fence enclosing plain modern houses.

A little patch of blue next to the fence caught my eye. I walked over to it.

It was a single bluebell plant, its bell-shaped

flowers bowing to the ground.

I dropped to my knees and buried my face in the cluster of bells. And as I inhaled their lovely rich scent, I was transported back to the bluebell wood, in my long cotton dress and leather boots, breathing the flower-scented air, marvelling at the shimmering haze of colour that stretched into the distance like a magic purple lake.

Where had all the bluebells gone?

Buried under concrete, under the foundations of houses. Suffocated, stifled, shrivelled to nothing.

And suddenly, like a blow to the stomach, it struck me properly for the first time.

Sophia was dead. Polly was dead. Robbie was dead. Nothing would be left of them but skeletons in the ground.

I curled up in a ball on the grass and cried until I had no tears left.

CHAPTER THIRTY-THREE

A Time to Seek

I woke in the chill of a grey afternoon, stiff and frozen to the bone.

I opened my eyes. There was the grass and the fence and the single bluebell plant.

A violent shudder went through me. I heaved my stiff cold body off the ground and hobbled into the house.

Back in my bedroom, I traced the writing on the window with my fingers. It was my only link to the past. Everything else had changed. The door was different, the fireplace had gone, there was a different rug on the floorboards.

I drew in my breath.

The floorboards!

What if...?

Heart hammering, I pushed back the bed.

And there it was. The floorboard that was shorter than the others.

The nails at each corner looked as though they weren't quite as tightly fixed as those in the surrounding boards. It wasn't something you would notice unless you were looking for it, but they definitely looked a tiny bit higher.

It would only be an empty box. But it would be something. It would prove that it had all been real. And it would be something to keep. Sophia would have wanted me to have it, I was sure.

I fetched a knife from the kitchen, knelt on the floor and pushed the blade under the head of the nearest nail. I thought it would come up easily, as it seemed to have done for Sophia. But the nail was stuck fast. Had Sophia been stronger than she looked?

Then I remembered. The nails had probably not been disturbed for two hundred years.

I rummaged in the kitchen utensil drawer and found a flat metal tool, the sort you use to turn roast potatoes. But the metal was too thick to fit under the nail. I had to slide the knife under and chip away at the wood until I had made a gap deep enough to wedge the tool underneath. Then, using all my strength, I pushed on the other end.

And the nail started to move. Millimetre by millimetre, it rose from the wood until, with one final push on the lever, it flew into the air and landed with a ping on the other side of the room.

Trying to stay calm, I turned my attention to the second nail. With the same painstaking effort, I prised it out of the board. Then the third. After what seemed like forever, the final nail came out.

My hands shook as I squeezed my fingertips into the gaps at either end of the floorboard. I screwed my eyes shut. If the gap between the joists turned out to be empty, I didn't think I could bear the disappointment.

Keeping my eyes shut, I lifted the board out and laid it on the floor. Then I took a deep breath and forced myself to look.

It was still there.

Coated with dust, it sat snugly in the gap between the joists, just where I had watched Sophia replace it before she had left Charlbury forever.

I sat there, smiling and smiling at the dusty wooden box. I couldn't believe it was still there. For two hundred years, it had sat under these floorboards, quietly gathering dust, while people lived their lives around it, never knowing it existed. It was amazing to think that the last time it had been touched was when Sophia took out the bracelet that would enable her and Robbie to start a new life together. And I had been there with her, standing in this exact spot, two hundred years ago. Or a week ago, depending on how you looked at it.

So it really had all been true. I would never have to doubt my sanity again. I had proof. And it was something I could keep forever, to remind me of my ancestors.

A thrill like electricity ran through me as I lifted it out and set it gently on the floor. It was surprisingly heavy.

I opened the lid, and my mouth fell open.

Because the box wasn't empty.

It was stuffed full of papers. And on top of the papers sat an old book.

I stared at it, frowning in bemusement. Who had put these things here?

I took out the book, set it aside and looked at the envelope on top of the pile of papers. There was one word written on the front.

Evie.

CHAPTER THIRTY-FOUR

A Time
to Keep

With trembling hands, I picked up the envelope. The paper was thick and smooth. The name was written in black ink, in neat sloping handwriting.

I knew that writing.

Feeling light-headed, I opened the envelope and unfolded the sheet of cream-coloured paper inside it. The paper was covered in the same handwriting.

My dear Evie,

If you are reading this, I shall be so happy, since it will mean that you are alive and well. My beloved husband and I have searched for you in every way we could think of, and this is my last, desperate attempt to contact you. I thought there might be a slight possibility that, since the house is now shut up and deserted, with only the butler and housekeeper resident, you might one day be tempted to return to Charlbury and retrieve this box.

You might not even know that, thanks to your ingenuity and courage, Robbie and I did successfully elope and were married at Gretna Green. We travelled back to London, sold my dear grandmother's bracelet and rented a little house. We took my grandmother's surname, Cranfield, in gratitude to her. Only then did we have time to reflect on the extraordinary sacrifice you made for us. I realised, with horror, that I had been so absorbed in my own situation that I had allowed you to sacrifice your freedom, and quite possibly your life, for my own selfish ends.

We made enquiries through Robbie's aunt Elizabeth in the village, but it appeared that nobody knew what had become of you. "Sophia" had vanished without a trace. Rumours were in circulation that she had died in her room, even that my father had murdered her. Yet George, the footman, told Elizabeth that my father was unwell on the night you disappeared and that he and Mr Paxton had been attending to him almost constantly. He is certain that "Sophia" somehow managed to escape from the locked room.

I cannot conceive of how you were able to effect this extraordinary feat, but the fact that you achieved it is one more example of your bravery. Your strength of character and selflessness, dear Evie, have been an inspiration to my husband and me throughout our lives. We always felt that we must achieve something worthwhile to honour your sacrifice.

As we had promised we would, we dedicated our lives to campaigning to improve the appalling lot of children in this country. I have placed in this box a copy of our little book, which, along with the far greater works of Mr Dickens, Mr Kingsley and many others, had some small effect in changing the laws of the country to improve the terrible plight of millions of children.

My darling husband passed away last year, after a short illness. He and I were twin souls, and I grieve for him more than I can express. But our dear son, Theodore, has, now that we are well out of danger, reverted to his father's name, Tregarron. Since Robbie was the only person in the world with that name, we particularly wished it not to die out. I am fortunate enough to be blessed with a beautiful grandson, Arthur, who will continue the name into the future.

When I reflect upon my life before my marriage, I marvel that I was able to summon up the courage to defy my father and elope with Robbie. It was only through your extraordinarily noble help and support, dear Evie, that I was able to do so. My life as Sophia Cranfield has been so rich and full of adventure. I tremble to think what my life as Mrs Charles Ellerdale would have been. Yet so very many women, rich and poor alike, lead such lives of fear and misery. There is much work left to do.

I wish so very much that I could have found you, Evie. Robbie and I made enquiries through every avenue we could think of. We even took out an advertisement in The Times to try to trace you. But none of our enquiries produced any fruit. It was as though you had vanished from the face of the earth. It did not help, I suppose, that we never were able to discover your surname. Mrs Hardwick, who had engaged you and must have known your full name, left Charlbury soon after you did. She provided no forwarding address. And the strangest thing was that when George looked in the housekeeper's records, which Mrs Hardwick kept meticulously, there was no trace of your name. It was as though you had never been at Charlbury.

I know it is probably foolish to hope that you will return and look for the box, but I have made this one last journey back, to put these things here, just in case. Along with the book are some newspaper clippings – reviews of the book and reports of our campaigning work – the work that you made possible when you helped us to escape.

I hope so very much that you have led a happy and fulfilling life, dear Evie. I am an old lady now, and you, I suppose, are an old lady too. It is strange, but although I know I have aged, I cannot imagine that you have done so at all. I still picture you as the girl of thirteen whom I knew for a brief time all those years ago.

If you are reading this, dear Evie, then you have fulfilled my final wish.

Yours ever,
Sophia

Charlbury, 24th April 1870

Sitting on the bed, I read the letter over and over again.

Somehow, this made everything different. Sophia

had reached out to me from the past. Two hundred years after we met, we could still communicate with each other.

Once I had read the letter so many times that I almost knew it by heart, I folded it up again and carefully slid it back into the envelope. Then I picked up the pale-blue hardback book that had lain on top of the letter. I read the title and the authors' names.

LOST IN THE CITY
ROBERT AND SOPHIA CRANFIELD

I opened the book and my heart leapt as I saw the illustration on the title page. It was the drawing Robbie had given Sophia in the stable yard on the first day I met him: the picture of two exhausted, starving children, dressed in rags.

I turned the page. The next was blank, apart from one line of text in the centre.

For Evie, wherever she may be

CHAPTER THIRTY-FIVE

A Time to Heal

Drowsily, I fumbled for the clock and switched off the alarm. It was 11.55pm. I had set the alarm before I went to sleep. I just needed to be sure.

I sat up in bed and waited for the living-room clock to strike. As the twelfth stroke of midnight died away, I listened intently.

Outside, an owl hooted. I heard the creak of bedsprings as Anna moved in her sleep. I continued to wait, but nothing changed. There was no tapping on the windowpane. No sound from the stable clock. Everything was normal.

I walked to the window and opened the curtains. My reflection stared back at me. I lifted my arm. My reflection did the same. I reached up to draw the curtains together again, and my reflection reached up too.

I smiled as I closed the curtains, and my reflection smiled back.

CHAPTER THIRTY-SIX

Home

The carrier bags dug into my hands as I walked home from the shops. As well as the basic groceries, I had bought everything I could think of that Mum might like: chocolates, peanut butter, cheese, grapes. Even, for some reason, a pineapple.

When I had left home five days ago, it had felt like winter. Now spring seemed to have arrived all at once. It was warm and sunny, with fluffy clouds floating high in the blue sky. The cherry trees along our street were all in bloom, and tulips and narcissi brightened the front gardens.

I walked past the garage forecourt, where plastic sacks of coal were stacked against the wall. That would be a nice surprise for Mum.

The woman at the counter looked at me doubtfully.

"Are you with someone? In a car?"

"No," I said. "I'm walking."

She looked at the carrier bags in my hands. "How are you going to get it home then?"

"Don't worry," I said. "I'll manage."

I clutched the sack of coal against my chest with both arms, with the shopping bags dangling from my wrists. It was lucky I didn't have far to go.

I turned off the main road into a side street, and sat on a low garden wall to rest for a minute. I leaned the coal against the wall and eased the carrier bags off my sore wrists. At least my hands were healing.

The wall belonged to a tall, old house with long sash windows. A date was carved into the stone above the front door. 1792.

So this house had been here when Robbie and Sophia were alive. This part of London would have been a village in those days, surrounded by fields. Maybe Robbie and Sophia had come up here sometimes, on a rare day when they weren't campaigning, or writing their book, or lobbying Parliament to introduce universal education. Maybe they had walked past this very house.

I looked at the worn stone step in front of the garden gate. Generations of family and servants and visitors must have crossed that threshold. How many thousands, millions, of footsteps did it take to wear a groove that deep in a slab of stone?

From the papers in my box, I had discovered that Robbie and Sophia's book, the story of two brothers apprenticed to a chimney sweep, had caused a sensation. It had helped to change attitudes to child labour, and eventually helped to change the law.

A breeze blew across the pavement. Something sparkled in the sunlight. A spider's web, suspended between the gatepost and a bush. A huge, perfect web, moving backwards and forwards in the breeze, stretching and bending, but never breaking. Fat little dewdrops perched on the almost invisible threads, perfectly balanced, a tiny rainbow held in every minuscule sphere.

I crouched in front of the web, marvelling at the miracle of it, at the threads that looked so fragile, that individually could be destroyed in an instant by a careless hand, but were stronger than steel when woven together. I took from my shoulder bag a little notebook and pencil.

As I crouched there, sketching the spider's web, a robin fluttered down from a bush and perched on the wall, its head on one side, the round black eyes looking enquiringly at me.

"Hello," I whispered. "Hello, little robin."

The robin hopped off the wall into the garden. I looked at my watch. I had three hours before Mum and Marcus would be home from the airport.

I stood up, put the notebook back in my bag, looped the carrier bags over my wrists and picked up the sack of coal.

"Right," I said to no one in particular. "Home."

Back at the flat, I went into action. I started as Polly had taught me, by dusting the surfaces, beginning at the top shelves and working my way down. I cleaned the bathroom until it sparkled, revelling in the luxury of rubber gloves and unlimited running water. Then I hoovered the entire flat, smiling as I thought how Polly would have loved this incredible machine that sucked up dust and dirt without you ever having to work on your hands and knees. I vacuumed up the dust from the long-neglected fireplace and took out all the pine cones that had been sitting in the grate for as long as I could remember. They would make perfect kindling.

It was amazing how different it felt doing housework in my own home, for somebody I loved. I wondered whether Polly had ever had her own home, or whether she had spent her whole life working for other people. We hadn't been able to get an appointment at the records office yesterday, but Anna had promised to go when she had the chance. It had been quite tricky explaining why I was so interested in researching the life of a random housemaid from two hundred years ago.

"I just read the names of some of the servants in that book you've got about the history of the house," I said, hoping she wouldn't check. (I actually had looked in the book, but none of the servants were mentioned.) "This girl, Polly Harper, was the same age as me when she worked here, and I thought it would be interesting to know more about her."

Anna had looked approving. "Well, I'm delighted you're interested in the history of the place," she said. "It's always difficult, though, to find anything out about servants apart from birth, marriage and death dates. They left so little trace of their lives, you see. Before universal education, few of them would have been able to read or write, and even if they could, they didn't have the time. They would have had hardly any possessions, and those they did have rarely survived."

"What about the housekeeper's book?" I asked.

"If the household records have survived," she said, "there should be an entry stating when Polly began and finished her employment here. But Charlbury's records were probably lost or destroyed when the house changed ownership, or when it was converted into flats."

There must have been millions of people like Polly, I thought now, as I cleaned the kitchen sink. Millions of people who spent their entire lives working to make other people's lives easier, who left no record of their own lives because they had never been taught to write, and who lay in unmarked graves because their families couldn't afford a private burial.

I laid the fire with paper, coal and pine cones, and lit it, marvelling, after all my struggles with flint and steel, at the ease of striking a match against a box. The fire crackled into life and I left it to settle while I arranged fruit in a bowl, tulips in a vase and cheese on a plate.

My phone – which had miraculously come back from the dead on the journey home – beeped with an email. It was from Anna.

Dear Evie,

I thought you'd like to know that I went to the records office this morning after dropping you at the station and had some success with my research into Polly Harper. Luckily, many of Charlbury's household records from the nineteenth century have survived and are held in the archive.

Polly arrived at Charlbury in 1812, aged eleven, and worked as a housemaid until 1820. In that year, she married one of the footmen, George Lewis, and they left Charlbury to become housekeeper and butler in a house in Highfield. So Polly did very well for herself.

Do come back and stay at any time, if you'd like to research more of the house's history. I'd be very happy to help in any way I can.

I hope your journey home went smoothly. Give my love to your mother – and try to be nice to the husband.

Anna

PS Thank you for the chocolates you left in your room – they're delicious. But did you mean to leave me a pair of washing-up gloves too? Were they supposed to be a hint? I'll save them for your next visit!

I read the email twice, smiling at the screen. So Polly did achieve her dream. She must have taught herself to read and write using the primer I left under the pillow. And she married George too! As butler and housekeeper, they would have had their own apartment in the house in Highfield. So when I thought about her from now on, I could picture her sitting contentedly in her own room, with a roaring fire and an endless supply of the family's tea.

Feeling very happy, I started to type a reply.

Dear Anna,

Thank you for your email and thank you so much for finding out about Polly. I'm so pleased she became a housekeeper. Thank you for having me to stay too.

I looked up from the screen, pondering what to write next.

I wondered what had happened to Jacob and Alice and Mary and Betty and William and Nell. I wondered if the records of that house in Highfield where Polly became a housekeeper were also in the archive. Perhaps I could find out more about her life after she left Charlbury.

Maybe one day I could write a history of Charlbury House. It would be way more interesting than that dull old pamphlet in Anna's flat. I could write about what had happened to Sophia and Robbie after they left. I could write about the staff who actually ran the house, not just the people they worked for. And I could write in great detail about a particular few days in April 1814.

I could illustrate the book as well. Sophia had left some sketches of hers and some of Robbie's in my box. I could put them in my book, and I could do some of my own too.

An extraordinary thought suddenly hit me for the first time. Charlbury had been my family's house.

I would be writing the history of my own family house. How incredible was that?

I hadn't told Anna about the box yet. I wanted it to be my secret for a while. But I would show it to her some day. And I would show Mum too. After all, Robbie and Sophia were her ancestors as well.

I would never show anyone my letter from Sophia, though. That would be my secret forever.

I went back to my email.

It would be great to come back and learn more about the history of the house. I'd like to draw it too. Maybe I can come in half term, if that's OK with you?

Thanks again and hopefully see you soon. Have fun with the skeletons.

Evie

The doorbell rang. I ran down the stairs and unlocked the front door.

"Mum!"

"Evie! Oh, it's so lovely to see you."

She almost squeezed me to death in an enormous hug. So she hadn't completely replaced me with Marcus then.

Once I was able to disentangle myself, I looked up the garden path.

"Where's Marcus?"

"He's popped in to work to sort out a couple of things," she said.

"Oh, right."

I was almost disappointed not to see him. I'd been quite looking forward to showing off my work.

"I think he was being tactful," Mum said. "Giving you and me a bit of time together first." She looked at me anxiously. "So try to be nice to him, Evie."

"Of course I'll be nice to him," I said. "What do you think I am?"

I picked up her suitcase.

"I'll take it," she said. "It's heavy."

"It's fine," I said. "I can carry a suitcase, you know. How was Venice?"

"Gorgeous," said Mum as she followed me up the stairs. "I'll tell you all about it once I've made a cup of tea. Sorry you had to come home to such a mess. I just didn't have time to clean before we went away, what with all the wedding preparations. I'll do it tomorrow."

I opened the door of the flat. Mum sniffed the air. "Has someone been cleaning?"

"Yes," I said. "I have."

Mum looked astounded. "You cleaned the flat?"

"Well, don't sound so surprised."

"But … I thought you'd only just got back."

"I came home a bit earlier. I wanted to get things ready for you. Come and see."

Mum looked at me in wonder. I led her in to the living room. Her jaw actually dropped.

"A fire! You've lit the fire! And candles! And look at those beautiful flowers! And it all looks so clean! Did you really do all this yourself?"

"Do you like it?"

"I love it! It looks absolutely gorgeous. My goodness," she said, walking over to the mantelpiece, "have you polished the candlesticks?"

"I found some Brasso in the cupboard."

"I can't even remember when I last polished those. They were your grandmother's. They look stunning. And you've polished the door handles too! And the window catches."

She stared at me.

"I can't believe you've done all this. Where did you learn to make a fire?"

I shrugged. "I just learned a bit – being at Charlbury – about how people used to live, you know? With fires and candles and stuff. And it's made me appreciate things more."

Mum frowned, as though she couldn't make sense of this. "You learned that from staying at Anna's? But it's all been converted into flats, hasn't it? I shouldn't have thought there's much left now of how the place used to be."

"Oh," I said, "you'd be surprised. It's amazing how much of the past is still there, if you look in the right places."

Acknowledgements

This book was inspired by the lives of many real people and places, and particularly by the story of the elopement and subsequent imprisonment of Hetty Walwyn, at Hellens Manor in Herefordshire. I am very grateful to the trustees of Hellens Manor for allowing Nosy Crow to take photographs at the house.

Thanks to Joe Friedman, Candy Gourlay, Paolo Romeo and Christina Vinall, for critiquing early drafts and encouraging me to continue. Huge thanks to Cliff McNish, who read an entire draft and sent me such thoughtful and helpful comments. Enormous thanks to Nino Cirone, for generously reading several drafts and guiding me in the right direction.

I am so lucky that my books are published by the fabulous team at Nosy Crow. Thank you so much for everything you do. Thanks especially to my wonderful editor, Kirsty Stansfield, for your invaluable advice, enthusiasm and encouragement.

I am immensely grateful to my lovely children, Dorothea and Freddy, who kindly allowed me to read them several drafts of this book, and gave incredibly helpful (if occasionally painful) feedback.

Lastly, and always, thanks most of all to Oliver, who helped me find the story and who always believed in it.